One
more piece.
Archimedes'
precious gear.
And then it all
could truly begin.
And end.
Spectacularly.

CAHILLS vs. VESPERS

DAY OF DOOM

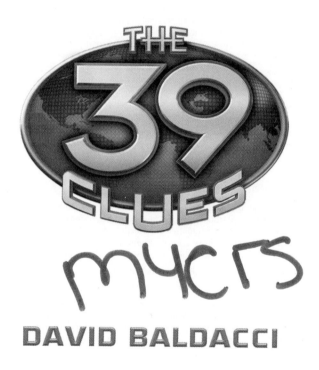

THE 39 CLUES

mycrs

DAVID BALDACCI

SCHOLASTIC INC.

To Spencer, Collin, Zoe, and Luke,
enjoy the ride
— D.B.

Library of Congress Control Number: 2012948468

ISBN 978-0-545-29844-5
10 9 8 7 6 5 4 3 2 1   13 14 15 16 17/0

Book design by SJI Associates, Inc.
Book illustrations by Cheung Tai and SJI Associates, Inc. for Scholastic. Compass p. 46:
Division of Political History, National Museum of American History, Smithsonian
Institution; case pp. 46, 136, and 165: wood textures from CG textures; banner p. 115:
photo by Ken Karp for Scholastic; back endpaper photo: character photo by Ken Karp
for Scholastic and background from CG textures.

First edition, March 2013

Printed in China 62

Scholastic US: 557 Broadway • New York, NY 10012
Scholastic Canada: 604 King Street West • Toronto, ON M5V 1E1
Scholastic New Zealand Limited: Private Bag 94407 • Greenmount, Manukau 2141
Scholastic UK Ltd.: Euston House • 24 Eversholt Street • London NW1 1DB

A	(	**O**	
E		**R**	
H		**S**	
M	●	**T**	
N		**U**	

CHAPTER 1

The etched glass goblet sat on an exquisite marble countertop. The countertop was in the bathroom of a luxurious hotel room. The hotel room was in New York City, where luxurious hotel rooms are fairly common. The goblet looked like a reproduction antique that one might find in an eight-hundred-dollar-a-night deluxe room at the Ritz-Carlton.

Only the goblet wasn't a beautiful reproduction. The hotel hadn't placed it there. Someone else had.

And the goblet wasn't empty. It was, in fact, about to be used.

The boy reached down and gripped the goblet. In it was the potion he'd completed, a mass of reddish-green liquid that pooled in the glass container like a deadly slime about to be unleashed on the world — a description that was not so far off the mark. He lifted the goblet and touched it to his lips, and then tipped it back. The contents slipped past his lips, entered his mouth, and washed down his throat and into his belly. He gave a small shudder as the foul concoction landed firmly in his gut and his taste buds roared their disapproval.

Dan Cahill wiped off his mouth with the back of his hand, a hand that was beginning to shake. He set the goblet down on the counter. He had selected the ornately carved goblet because what he had just done was a momentous act, and he had wanted to do it in style.

He had thought long and hard before doing what he had just done. But Dan ultimately had decided that this was the only way. He walked into the living room of his suite and sat down in a plush chair, his focus completely on the empty goblet, which he could just make out through the open door. He cast his mind back to the time he had spent at Columbia University, more specifically in the science lab there. That's where, with the help of an Ekat scientist, he had manufactured this serum. Or *the* serum, rather. There was no other one like it in the world.

It hadn't been easy. Normally, creating the serum would require lots of time, money, and a lab beyond even what was available at Columbia. But Dan had been obsessed with producing the serum for a long time. Thus he had figured out some shortcuts in how to process it. He had always thought he might have to make the stuff while on the road. And, as it turned out, he'd been right.

He stared down at his hands. He had a reasonable idea of how long the interaction would take. Yet he was unsure of exactly what the transformation would be.

Will I turn into something like the Hulk? Big and green and possibly psycho?

A sense of panic started to leach into his brain, working its way down his spine, neuromuscular messages firing off to the rest of his body like an old-timey telegraph operator performing his dots-and-dashes SOS.

Am I in trouble? What did I just do? But what choice did I have?

Dan and his sister, Amy, had just handed their archnemesis the last elements needed to build a device that might end the world. And that outcome had taken a large psychological toll on both of them, but especially Amy. Dan and Amy had been through a lot, but Dan had never seen his sister withdraw like she had over the last twenty-four hours. He wasn't even sure that she could continue on as the leader of the Cahills. And if she couldn't, who could?

Maybe me. Maybe I'm it.

So really, what choice did I have?

The answer was painfully obvious.

None.

So he sat and waited for the serum to bring him the physical strength of a superhero and the turbo-charged mental prowess of a thousand Einsteins. He could almost sense the power wave rushing at him. He stood and looked in a mirror bolted to the wall. He did this not simply because he wanted to see the transformation as it was happening. He also wanted to do this because Dan Cahill was about to disappear forever. He wanted to see himself one last time, before he became something else irreversibly.

There was also the other thing. He had no idea what the serum would really do to him. It might end up killing him. Only one person had ever taken the stuff, and that had been over five centuries ago. What Dan desperately wanted — indeed, the only reason why he had gathered the necessary ingredients and concocted the formula — was to have the serum convey on him extraordinary powers, both physically and intellectually, with which to fight and beat the Vespers. But they might come at an enormous cost. It might be that the human body was not built to contain such forces, at least not for long. But Dan didn't need to be super forever. He just needed it long enough to defeat the Vespers, rescue the hostages, and save the world.

It was a short, though substantial, bucket list.

I am willing to die for this. He mouthed the words, so he could see himself saying them in the mirror. *This is the end for me.* It was heady stuff for a thirteen-year-old with his whole life ahead of him.

Well, my life just got a whole lot shorter. But it's okay. It will be worth it.

He felt noble. He felt right.

He also felt nothing happening.

He stared more closely at the mirror. Same hair, same height, same bone structure. His skin was not turning green. He did not look the least bit psycho.

Massive muscles were not plating themselves on top of his normal ones. He checked his watch. Twenty minutes had passed. And nothing. Something was wrong. Something was terribly freaking wrong. Had he not done the formula correctly? Had one of his shortcuts ruined the whole process? But he'd been *sooo* careful.

Right then she stepped from the shadows thrown by a bulky armoire set against a far corner of the room.

His sister, Amy, sixteen years old and the de facto leader of the Cahill clan, looked back at him. She was tall and pretty and unbelievably smart. And she could kick butt, too. Dan loved her. Admired her. Looked up to her. But he was also her younger brother, so it was sort of his job to make her life slightly miserable from time to time.

But Amy was a shade of her former self. Before, she had been so resilient. She had taken blow after blow and come back strong. But this time was different. Now Amy had crawled in a shell that seemed so thick and strong she might never be free of its embrace. Dan was surprised that she had even come out of her room.

"What's up, Amy?" he said casually, sliding over and trying to block her view of the goblet through the opening into the bathroom. "You feeling better?"

"I'm sorry," she said.

"Sorry about what?"

"For acting like a wuss. For crawling inside myself because it seemed like the Vespers had won. But I'm back now, Dan. I'm ready to take up the fight. I won't let you and the others down like that again. This is a fight we all have to finish, and we're going to do it together."

Dan couldn't keep from smiling. This was the Amy he had been waiting for. No matter how tough things got, she always came back. But then he felt immediate guilt and more than a little panic. He'd already taken the serum.

As though reading his mind, she quickly moved to the side and glanced at the goblet through the bathroom doorway and then at her brother. Her look was a guilty one, yet her lips were set in a firm line. Dan sensed that she was about to make *his* life miserable.

She said in a halting voice, "I couldn't let you do it, Dan. I just couldn't."

It took a long moment for Dan to process her words. When he finally did, he blurted out, "What did you do?"

"I found out what you were doing at Columbia. So when you were busy in your bedroom I slipped in the bathroom and substituted a puree of beets, brussels sprouts, and collard greens for the serum in the goblet. I poured the real serum down the drain," she said, her voice sounding even guiltier. "I couldn't let you do it. You could die."

Dan looked aghast. "A puree of beets, brussels sprouts, and collard greens? Were you trying to poison me?"

"Oh, come on. I was pretty sure the real serum would taste bad, so I couldn't exactly make it taste like a Dairy Queen Blizzard."

"We're all going to die now, thanks to you," snapped Dan.

"No, we're not. There's another way."

"There is *no* other way," Dan shouted, his eyes wet with tears. "I was prepared to do this, Amy. I *wanted* to do this. I was willing to die. I made the choice. Do you know how hard that was? And now, because of you, it was for nothing!"

She drew closer to him but did not reach out to him, sensing perhaps that this gesture would be unwelcome. "You are so brave, Dan. A lot braver than I am."

"Don't say stuff to try and make me feel better," her brother shot back. "It won't work."

"I need you, Dan. I need you with me." She pointed to the goblet. "It can do things to your mind. We both know that once you take the serum all bets are off. You might end up doing the very opposite of what you planned. It's just too dangerous."

"It was our only shot." Dan collapsed on the couch and touched his forehead to his knees. "It was the only way, Amy," he moaned. "And you ruined it."

She sat next to him and put an arm around his quaking shoulders. "No, it's not the only way. I told you, I'm back. I'm ready to take on the Vespers again. But I need your help."

He glanced up and eyed her suspiciously. "Are you telling me you really have a plan?"

"Look." She held up her phone. "I just got an e-mail from Ian and Evan. They've found out something extraordinary. In fact, it might be the very lead we need to beat the Vespers. It's one of the reasons why I came out of my room. It's why I think we have a shot."

"What is it?"

She drew a deep breath and said, "Isabel Kabra is Vesper Two."

Dan looked dumbstruck. "Not Vesper One?"

"No, at least not yet. I think we both know that playing second fiddle to anyone is not what Isabel is about. And Evan also hacked into her private jet's flight plans." She paused and added dramatically, "Isabel is flying to DC."

Dan sat up straighter. The tears were gone from his eyes and he fully focused on his sister. "Washington? Why?"

"That's what we have to find out. That's why I've called a meeting."

"A meeting? With who?"

There was a knock on the hotel room door. Amy rose, checked the peephole, and opened it. Atticus and Jake Rosenbloom were standing there. Atticus was close to Dan's age and short. Jake was eighteen, tall, and good-looking.

"Them," said Amy. "So are you with me, Dan?"

Dan stood up and walked toward her, his anger at his sister gone.

"I'm with you, sis. To the end."

CHAPTER 2

The door was closed and locked. Dan and Amy, and Jake and Atticus Rosenbloom, sat around on the floor, discussing their plan and scarfing room service. Dan was devouring a loaded cheeseburger with fries, while Atticus was spooning soup into his mouth. Jake was finishing his pizza. Amy had gotten a salad, but had eaten half of Dan's fries. Grease was apparently wonderful fuel for plotting against evil.

Their dilemma was an obvious one for Amy and Dan. They had been engaged in it for a very long time. That came with being part of the Cahill family, which was the most powerful family in the world. Over the centuries their members had included some of the most famous people of all time: politicians, scientists, explorers, athletes, soldiers, and the list went on and on. There was not one category of human history that had not in some way been touched by a Cahill.

Facing off against the Cahills was a group of nearly equal potency but with tons of evil thrown in.

The Vespers.

They were a centuries-long chain of people committed to bending the world and all those who lived there to their will. The Vespers naturally saw the Cahills as their sworn enemies and the epic confrontations between the two clans had been going on for a very long time. The Vespers had recently gained the upper hand, forcing Amy and others to do their bidding by kidnapping a number of their friends and family members. If the Vespers were not given the items they demanded, many of which had required Amy and her friends to break into important institutions and steal various items — including priceless works of art — then the hostages would be killed.

Now that all the items had been delivered to the Vespers, not a single one of the hostages had been released. Indeed, the Cahills had just figured out that the Vespers were planning to use the stolen items to construct some sort of Doomsday machine. That's what they were trying to prevent. And they also needed to find and rescue the hostages before the Vespers killed them. None of it would be easy. Some of it might be impossible.

But Cahills never gave up, regardless of the odds against them.

Amy put down her fork and said, "Okay, let's just get everything straight. The Vespers have all the elements they need to build the Doomsday device. There can be no doubt of that."

Jake added, "Right. The last pieces were the ring-slash-gear thing and the Siffright documents."

Amy found herself gazing longingly at Jake and felt her heart beating faster. He was so hot! And smart! And hot! But there was still Evan Tolliver. The fact was that Amy cared for them both. And she thought they both cared for her. She understood that at some point she would have to make a decision. She just wasn't prepared to do it now.

She peeked once more at Jake. But when she felt Dan's annoyed gaze on her she quickly got back her groove.

"Subduction zones," she announced. "That's the key. The Doomsday device will trigger some tectonic plate overload and the result will be Armageddon with thousands, maybe millions of people dead. Does everyone agree with that assessment?"

"Yes, even if it's nuts," said Jake. "The Vespers are seriously sick people."

"Tell us something we don't know," snapped Dan. He was obviously still feeling a bit ticked off because Amy had pulled the serum out from under him. "The Vespers *specialize* in grossly evil stuff. It should be their motto. 'Grossly Evil for Hire. World Destruction at Good Rates.'"

"Look, there's no reason to get upset with each other," said Amy, looking at Dan with a guarded expression. "We have to work *together* to get this done."

"No argument there," said Jake, who now gazed

longingly at Amy. He was clearly as smitten with her as she was with him.

Dan caught this look and seemed ready to throw up. "Okay," he said. "We know what *they* have. We know what *they* want to do. We know that *they* are not going to release the hostages even though we did what they asked us to, because they're slimy, stinking, lying Vespers. Now the question is: What do *we* do to stop them?"

The next comment came from Atticus. Eleven-year-old Atticus Rosenbloom didn't much look like the last person left on earth whose task was to save the world from destruction. He was small and sort of puny, but his brain was big and muscular and operating on about a 200 IQ. And he'd recently found out that he was the world's last remaining Guardian, one of a group dedicated to keeping the Doomsday machine out of the wrong hands, meaning the Vespers' hands.

Atticus said, "I just remembered something my mother told me. I've been racking my brains for a long time now, trying to think of anything she said that might help us."

His mother, Astrid Rosenbloom, a renowned scholar, had recently died. That was the awful bond that he and Dan shared—losing their mothers. Dan and Amy's parents had died in a fire set by Isabel Kabra, who seemed to be competing neck-and-neck with Vesper One for the title of "Most Evil Person Alive."

"What?" asked Dan. "What did she say?"

"It was when she was so ill and delirious. She kept

gripping my hands and mentioning the name 'Lewis' and the name 'Clark.' She did it over and over. At first I thought they were doctors who were treating her when she was so sick. But then it just occurred to me that when you put their names together—"

Amy broke in. "Lewis and Clark, the explorers!"

"Right," said Atticus.

"Okay," said Jake. "But how do Lewis and Clark help us? They've been dead a long time. What could they possibly have to do with the Vespers and the Doomsday device?"

Atticus said, "But their work lives on. All the things they discovered. They're in displays at museums all over the country, probably."

Dan, who had gotten on his laptop and furiously clicked keys, looked up triumphantly. "And the largest collection of items gathered from the Lewis and Clark expedition is housed at the National Museum of American History."

Amy caught a breath. "And that's in DC."

"Where Isabel Kabra is heading right now," added Dan gleefully.

"Which means that's where we're headed, too," replied Amy. "And if we're lucky, we can nail Isabel in the process. If we do that, then maybe the entire Vesper plan collapses."

"Do you really think so?" asked Jake doubtfully. "I mean, there are lots of other places Isabel could be traveling to in DC."

Amy gazed at him, not longingly this time, but sternly. "Yeah, I really do." She looked at everyone. "Start packing. We're outta here."

Everybody scattered to get ready for the trip. When he was alone, Dan got down on his knees and reached under the couch. He pulled out a silver flask. Inside it was a second dose of the serum. He had made two as a precaution. Not because he thought Amy would sabotage what he had done, but because it was always good to have a Plan B. The serum had a very odd smell, which he disguised by adding a handful of red M&Ms. It wouldn't do anything to adversely affect the serum, but it might make it taste better. He put the flask away in his knapsack.

As he finished packing, Dan's intentions were clear. If it came to it, he would still take the serum. If there was no other way for the Cahills to stop the Vespers, he would die trying. It was just how he was built. Sacrifice for the greater good was part of who he was, and who his sister was, too.

And next time, Dan would make sure that neither Amy nor anyone else would be able to stop him. He was going to beat the Vespers, even if it killed him.

He grabbed his bags, joined Amy and the others, and off they trudged to the train station to catch a ride to DC. And a possible confrontation with one of the deadliest, and meanest, people Dan had ever met.

You're going down this time, Isabel Kabra, thought Dan as he got in the cab.

CHAPTER 3

The breaths still came hard and fast for some. And the tears were still falling. Alistair Oh had been dead only a short time and the grief still lay heavy and hurtful over all the remaining hostages. Understanding death was always hard. Premature death in close proximity was harder still to comprehend.

Nellie Gomez rubbed her healing but still painful shoulder and brushed her filthy hair out of her face. It felt like years had passed since she had been snatched off the streets of Paris. She wasn't sure exactly how much time had elapsed, but she had a sinking feeling that the odds of their ending up as Alistair had were growing by the minute.

She looked around at the other hostages.

Reagan Holt, normally the Energizer Bunny of the Tomas clan, was sitting on her haunches staring at her dirty sneakers. It looked like her batteries had finally run out.

Natalie Kabra, the fashion queen of the Lucian branch, sat looking equally moody and depressed.

Nellie sort of blamed Natalie for her wound. After all, it had appeared the Vespers were going to shoot Natalie first, but a voice ordered them not to. So they had shot Nellie instead.

Thanks a lot, Nellie thought as she gazed with unfriendly eyes at Natalie. But then again, Isabel had also shot Natalie in the foot when they were all after the 39 Clues. And Natalie *had* managed to get the bullet out of Nellie's shoulder when Phoenix had failed to do so. Okay, she had been able to do it because she was a great eyebrow-plucker and could wield tweezers like nobody's business. And her eyes had been closed the entire time she'd searched for the bullet because she'd been totally grossed out by the gunshot wound. But still, she *had* gotten the bullet out.

And she's probably missing her brother, Ian, thought Nellie. *But I'm missing a lot of people, too.*

Nellie's gaze moved to the spot that Phoenix Wizard normally would have occupied. Phoenix had died while attempting to escape. At least he was free from the Vespers, but Nellie missed him a lot.

She next looked at Ted Starling. The teenager gazed at nothing, literally. Badly injured during an explosion when looking for the 39 Clues, Ted could see only light and dark, nothing else. But he was plucky and had held up as well as any of the hostages.

The only other adult hostage Nellie worried about was Fiske Cahill. He and Nellie were the guardians of Amy and Dan, and Fiske was the de facto head of the Madrigal branch and nearly seventy. Long known as the Man in Black, and a tough, tenacious dude, he looked, to Nellie, defeated.

I suppose I look beaten to everyone else, she thought.

Nellie was about to say something to Fiske when they heard the footsteps approach. Like wounded animals, each of the hostages instinctively hunkered down and slid as deeply into the shadows as they could. None of them ever took it as a good sign when that door opened.

All of them probably had the same thoughts running through their minds: *Is this it? Is today the day we die?*

The door swung open. A voice called out, "We're moving you. Get up!"

The hostages all slowly rose together as though tethered by rope.

Fiske Cahill said, "Where are we going?"

The voice said condescendingly, "What does it matter to you, old man?"

"Come close enough and I'll show you how well an old man can kick your butt."

Nellie smiled. Now *that* was the Fiske Cahill she hoped still existed.

The voice said, "But before we leave, you have one more thing to do."

"What?" blurted out Natalie.

"You get to say good-bye to your little friends, Amy and Dan Cahill."

This statement sent chills through all the hostages. Were they going to die? Or were Amy and Dan?

But one of them, Ted, saw an opportunity, even with his very bad eyesight.

The hostages trudged out of their prison, unsure of what the future would hold.

As Fiske Cahill passed one of the guards, the man said, "You talk big for an old fart." It was the same man who had told them they were moving.

"Big talk *this*," replied Fiske as he whipped around and landed a side kick right into the guard's gut, sending him flying back against the wall and slumping to the floor. Fiske bent down and whispered to the battered man, "That was for Alistair."

As other guards converged on him, Fiske straightened and said simply, "Terribly sorry about that. Lost my balance. Happens to old farts all the time."

He walked on, with his head held high.

CHAPTER 4

The command center in Attleboro was a lonely place. Only Ian Kabra and Evan Tolliver were there presently. They were both working hard, but they also felt disconnected from the action. And Ian was particularly gloomy because his sister was a hostage, and it didn't seem like there was any way to get her back.

Has my mother won? he thought.

Evan pounded his keyboard like some rocker pianist. He kept stopping to adjust his Coke-bottle glasses, which partially obscured his deep blue eyes. Evan lived for computers. In fact, he could not live without them.

He looked up. "Success!"

"What?" asked Ian.

"Hacked Sinead's e-mail account. Think I hit the jackpot. Well, at least it's something we didn't know before."

Ian looked over Evan's shoulder at the string of e-mails on the screen. He read quickly. "Right. Well now, she's e-mailed back and forth with this Riley McGrath chap." Ian read some more of the e-mails.

DAY OF DOOM

19

"He's a park ranger. Looks like she had a bit of a romantic thing for him. However, I'm not interested in Sinead's love life. And I don't quite see how that helps us."

While Ian had been reading, Evan had switched over to another computer.

"Here's how. I looked up Riley McGrath. Pretty difficult for him to be e-mailing Sinead."

"Why's that?"

"Because he's been dead for ten years."

As Ian stared quizzically at him, the cell phone they kept at the command center buzzed.

Ian looked at it. "I don't recognize that number."

"Better answer it," said Evan. "The only people who know this number are people we probably need to hear from."

Ian answered the phone. "Hello?"

"Who is this?" the voice asked. Ian thought he recognized it but wasn't sure.

"Who is *this*?" asked Ian.

"Is this Attleboro?"

Ian put the cell phone on SPEAKER so Evan could hear.

"Exactly who would like to know that information?" asked Ian in his stiffest British accent.

"This is Phoenix Wizard."

Ian and Evan gaped at each other. Could this really be Jonah's little cousin? It certainly sounded like him.

"Phoenix, Ian and Evan here," said Ian. "Can you tell us exactly where you are?"

Evan chimed in, "But first, are you all right?"

When Phoenix next spoke his voice was shaky and both Evan and Ian could hear tears behind the words.

"I almost got killed when I was escaping," Phoenix said. "It was really scary. I don't know how I made it through. I thought I was going to die."

Now both Ian and Evan could hear the little boy sniffling. Next a small sob escaped his lips.

"Right, Phoenix. This is Ian. I want you to take two deep breaths for me. Can you do that?"

"I can try."

"Good. Two deep ones. Let me hear them."

They heard two long breaths and then Ian said, "Brilliant, Phoenix. Best deep breaths I've ever heard. Now, I know your ordeal has been simply awful, but it would be very helpful if you could just pull yourself together and tell us what happened."

Evan added, "And that way we can come and help you, Phoenix."

"Precisely," said Ian. "You needn't be alone anymore. We will come to your aid with alacrity."

"That means really fast," said Evan, giving Ian an annoyed look.

After a few more sniffles and another long breath, Phoenix said, "After I escaped, I managed to get to a road. A man gave me a ride in his truck to a motel. I'm calling from there."

Something seemed to occur to Ian and his face turned ashen. "Right. But where are the others? Is my

DAY OF DOOM

21

sister, is she . . . ?" Ian shouted this last part into the phone.

Evan gripped his shoulder. "Just chill, dude. Let's hear what he has to say."

In a lower voice he said, "And let's verify it *is* Phoenix." In a louder voice he said, "Phoenix, what are your cousin's two favorite words?"

"*Word* and *bro*. With *yo* and *fly* close behind."

"That's Phoenix," said Ian.

Phoenix said, "I was able to get away from the Vespers. I'd been wandering through the mountains for a long time before I reached that road."

Evan said calmly, "We're really glad you're okay, Phoenix. But can you tell us exactly where you are?"

"In Washington State. Near the Cascade Mountain Range." He gave them the exact address of the motel. "If you get here, I can lead you to where the others are. I know right where it is."

Evan said, "Just hold tight, Phoenix. Hide as best you can. And don't talk to anybody. We'll be there as fast as the plane will take us."

Ian added in a nervous tone, "Phoenix, when you managed to escape, was everyone, was Natalie . . . ?" He again couldn't finish.

"They were all alive," said Phoenix.

"Okay, thanks," said Ian. "Thanks a lot."

As soon as the phone went dead, Evan fired off an e-mail to Amy telling her about the call. But it bounced back.

"Crap," snapped Evan. He tried again with the same result.

"I'll call her on the mobile," said Ian. But the call would not go through.

"What the heck is going on?" exclaimed Evan.

"We've got to reach Phoenix before the Vespers do," said Ian. "We'll try to contact the others on the way. Now let's jolly well get a move on."

In five minutes they were packed and out the door. Two hours later they were on a flight to the state of Washington.

CHAPTER 5

The Acela train was running smoothly on its way to DC. Amy, Dan, Jake, and Atticus were occupying a four-person table in one of the train cars. Dan had gone to the café car to get some food and had brought back snacks and drinks for the others. The room service meal seemed like a long time ago, though it really hadn't been. They were all at an age where the calories seemed to be burned up as soon as they passed the lips.

They had opted for the train because the earliest flight they could get out of New York would not have gotten them into DC faster than the train. And the train would carry them into Union Station, which was only a short cab ride away from the National Museum of American History.

Amy had just put down her bottle of water when her phone buzzed. She picked it up and looked at the incoming text. Her face froze.

Dan, who had been watching her, said, "Vesper One?"

She nodded and handed him the phone so the others could see the message.

Would you like to see the hostages one last time?

Vesper One had helpfully provided a password-protected link on the web.

Amy drew a long breath and readied her laptop. The train was full, so they decided to go out into the vestibule between train cars, where they could have some privacy. Amy carried her laptop while the others fell into step behind her. It was like they were marching to see an execution. The dread was clear on each of their faces.

They huddled in the vestibule while Amy hit the link on her computer screen and then put in the password.

They drew closer when the screen fired up, and the dread on their faces deepened.

The remaining hostages were lined up in a row. They looked dirty, beaten, battered. There was duct tape over their mouths and their hands were bound behind them.

Alistair wasn't there, of course, and neither was Phoenix. Amy and the others knew Alistair was dead and that Phoenix was missing and probably dead as well.

A robotic voice came on over the laptop's speaker. It was Vesper One. His tone was one of unabashed triumph.

"I just wanted to thank you for all of your help. I consider you my partners in bringing about the victory of my family over yours. Indeed, over the world. Without your valuable assistance in gathering the elements I needed, my plan would never have succeeded. I want you to keep that in mind over the short period of time you have left to live." The voice paused and then continued, "Oh, and in case you haven't figured it out for yourselves, I am officially going back on our deal to release the hostages once you provided me with all the elements. Lying is just what we Vespers do. And we do it so well. Makes life so much easier. Ciao."

They all looked at one another, the fury evident on each of their faces.

"I want to kill that guy," snapped Dan. "And then bring him back to life and kill him again. And keep doing it until he just disappears to *nothing*."

Unfortunately, he said all this right as a conductor walked by. When the man looked at him oddly, Dan pointed to the computer and said, "Uh, fantasy football league. My guy totally blew it."

"I feel your pain," said the conductor. "My guy threw four interceptions. I'm thinking about becoming a hockey fan."

As he walked off, Dan glanced back at the screen.

Atticus pointed at it. "Look."

They all stared at where he was pointing. The hostages couldn't say anything because of the duct tape. But their eyes were visible. And one of the hostages was doing something very interesting.

Ted Starling was blinking. But he was doing so in a highly unusual way.

It took Atticus a few moments to realize why. "He's blinking Morse code."

Atticus grabbed a notepad and pen from his jacket and watched the screen. "Amy," he said. "Back it up a little."

She did, and Atticus watched as Ted blinked and blinked and blinked.

Atticus started scribbling on his pad while the others watched.

When the screen finally went dark Amy said, "Did you figure it out?"

Atticus nodded. "I believe so." He looked at his notes and muttered, "Riley McGrath is Vesper One."

"Riley McGrath," said Dan. "Who's he?"

Amy said slowly, "I don't know."

"I wonder why Ted thinks he's Vesper One," said Atticus equally slowly, as though he was trying to answer the question before he finished saying it.

"I don't know," said Amy again. She suddenly looked sick to her stomach. "Excuse me," she said. She handed Dan her computer and slipped into the bathroom and shut and locked the door.

Jake glanced anxiously at Dan. "Do you think she's okay?"

"No, of course she's not okay," exclaimed Dan. "Alistair is dead. The hostages are still hostages. Phoenix is dead. And Vesper One basically told Amy that we were the ones responsible for destroying the world. After she's done in the bathroom, *I'm* going to go in there to throw up, too."

Dan slumped down to the floor and stared at his shoes.

"But at least we know Vesper One is Riley McGrath," pointed out Jake. "That's something."

"No. We just know that Ted *thinks* he is," replied Atticus. "That's not the same thing as it being a fact."

Dan said, "And how does that help us? We don't know who McGrath is and why Ted thinks he's Vesper One. We don't know where the hostages are located. For all we know they're already dead. That web link could be old. And now Vesper One has everything he needs to wreck the planet. Wow. Cool. Let's have a party."

Jake said angrily, "Hey, I know all that, okay? I'm just trying to stay positive."

"Don't bother," shot back Dan. "It just makes you look stupid, because there is nothing, absolutely nothing, to be positive about."

Jake was about to respond when the bathroom door slid back with a crash, making all three of them jump.

Amy stood there, a determined look on her face.

However, Dan did notice that her cheeks were red, her nose runny, and she looked like she had scrubbed her face hard to wipe away the tears.

"Okay, listen up, because here's the deal," she said. "All we can do is keep trying. Vesper One has the upper hand now. Alistair and Phoenix are dead. The hostages might be, too, soon. But we have a lead. We're going to follow that lead. If we can catch Isabel, we may have some bargaining power. And even if we don't, we can still find out what she wants in DC. That might help us somehow. I know it doesn't sound like much. But it's all we have right now. So we can sit around feeling sorry for ourselves, or we can keep fighting. I don't know about you, but I plan to keep fighting."

She took her laptop from Dan and marched back to her seat.

The guys all looked at one another.

"Wow," said Jake. "Not what I expected."

Dan said hotly, "What *did* you expect from her?"

"Well, she did sort of crack up about twenty-four hours ago," pointed out Atticus.

"Everybody is entitled to one meltdown," Dan said loyally. "But she's not going to give up again!"

"Hey, you sounded like *you* had given up," Jake reminded him.

Dan started to shout something back but stopped. "You're right. I did. But I was wrong," he said quietly.

Atticus added, "And the last thing we need is to start fighting with each other. We have plenty of bad people to fight as it is."

Jake said, "Atticus is right. I'm sorry, Dan." He put out his hand.

Dan shook it. "It's cool. Sometimes this fighting-global-evil-to-save-the-world thing starts to get a guy down."

Jake grinned. "I know exactly how you feel."

The three of them went off to join Amy in the fight.

CHAPTER 6

It was Dan who first noticed it. He'd been doodling on a napkin. Amy was surfing on her computer, no doubt trying to find some helpful lead or bit of information that would help them defeat the Vespers. Maybe she was looking at the floor plans for the Museum of American History in case they had to make an escape from it. It seemed to Dan that they could build a business out of escaping from museums, art galleries, and other secure places, seeing as how they had had to do it so often. Jake was leaning back in his chair staring at the ceiling. But he would occasionally glance over at Amy, and Dan would roll his eyes at the puppy-dog look Jake gave his sister. Atticus had his eyes closed, but Dan knew he wasn't sleeping. He was thinking. Atticus was always thinking. That came with having a brain the size of a watermelon.

So Dan had glanced out the window. They were, he thought, just passing over the Delaware River. But he wasn't looking at the river. He was looking at the sky. He sat up straighter and pressed his face to the window, his eyes pointed up at such a harsh angle they hurt.

Was the sky . . . purple?

And were the clouds actually moving that fast? It was like one of those zoom-track weather maps that accelerated the movements of storm and cloud patterns. But this was real. A second later a gust of wind hit the train so hard that it actually rocked back and forth. For a terrifying moment Dan thought that they were going to plummet into the water.

He looked around at the others. While they all seemed to have noticed the buffeting wind, they weren't looking outside. Dan glanced at some of the other passengers. They all were staring at their computers, or reading books or newspapers. Not one of them had noticed the weather. Maybe that's how the world was now, thought Dan. Everyone was so wrapped up in his or her own little world that no one ever really *saw* anything anymore.

"Uh, Amy," said Dan.

She looked up, obviously annoyed at this interruption.

"Yes?"

He pointed out the window.

She glanced past him. Her alarmed expression told Dan that she saw what he saw.

Now Jake and Atticus were looking out the window, too.

"The sky is . . . purple," said Jake. "How can the sky be purple?"

"Is there a rainbow somewhere around?" asked Atticus. "It might simply be a case of light refraction combined with other elements to create some sort of optical illusion."

"There's no rainbow," said Dan. "And since when have you seen clouds move that fast?"

They looked upward. The clouds flashed past and were soon out of sight.

They all looked at one another.

Amy said slowly, "It could be totally unrelated to the Doomsday device."

"Yeah," said Dan. "And I *could* actually be Justin Bieber, only with a better haircut."

"There's nothing we can do about it now," she said. "But we can try and narrow down the location of relevant subduction zones. That will tell us where the Vespers may have located the Doomsday device."

"Good idea," said Jake. "Let me help you." He was sitting next to Amy and simply eased up the armrest separating them and moved closer to her.

"Thanks, Jake," said Amy, smiling at him. "You're really good at helping."

Dan watched all this with an incredulous look. He really did want to throw up. He actually stuck a finger down his throat and made a gagging noise.

Amy ignored this and said, "Subduction zones, fortunately, aren't all that plentiful. And in the United

States they are pretty few in number. They're mostly along the coasts."

Atticus said, "That's still a lot of ground to cover. And we don't have much time." He looked out the window again and observed the ominous celestial happenings.

Amy's phone buzzed as an e-mail came in.

Dan looked at the device like it was a rattlesnake poised to plunge its fangs into him.

"Please don't let that be Vesper One telling us some-one else is dead," he muttered.

Amy picked up the phone. "It's from Evan." She read the e-mail and her jaw dropped nearly to the table. "Omigod."

"What is it?" asked Jake, who was trying to read the tiny screen.

Amy let out a long breath and tears filled her eyes. "Phoenix managed to escape from the Vespers. That's why he wasn't on the screen with the others."

Jake exclaimed, "Way to go, Phoenix!"

Amy looked at him. She didn't know Phoenix all that well. He had not been a big part of the Cahill family. But he was only twelve and Amy liked him, and when she had thought he was dead, she had felt tremendous guilt. Now she just felt stupendous relief.

"Where is he?" Dan asked quickly.

"At a motel near the Cascade Mountains in Washington State. Evan and Ian are on a plane right now to get him. Phoenix says he can lead them to the hostages. Evan sent me the address of the motel where they'll be. I'm going to e-mail him back now and tell him that he needs to get the police involved. I know that sort of goes against the Cahill way of doing things. But I'm afraid if they go after the hostages alone, they'll end up captured, too."

Dan said, "So we need to get on a plane and fly to Washington. Let's get off the train at the airport near Baltimore."

"No," said Amy. "We can't do that."

Dan looked stunned. "What are you talking about? Two minutes ago we had no clue where the Doomsday device was. Or where the hostages were. Now we know. The Cascades, I'm sure, has subduction zones."

Jake was hitting computer keys with dizzying speed. He read the screen and looked up. "There is an enormous subduction zone located right off the coast of Washington State," he said.

"Okay," said Dan triumphantly. "So we kill two birds with one stone. Doomsday device and the hostages. We're finally a step ahead of the Vespers. We have to go for it."

"What we have to do," countered Amy, "is find out why Isabel Kabra is going to DC."

"What does it matter?" exclaimed Dan. "And it might be a trap. Or this could just be a wild-goose chase."

"She had no reason to believe that we could hack into her files," pointed out Amy. "And why lead us on a wild-goose chase when, as far as she knows, we have no idea where the hostages or the Doomsday device are? If she's going to DC at such a critical time, it must be for a very good reason."

"I agree with Amy," said Jake.

"Of course you do!" snapped an exasperated Dan. "Because you're, like, so in loooove with her."

"Dan!" said Amy sharply, but she was also blushing.

Dan barked, "So we're just going to let Ian and Evan go in alone?"

"With the police," amended Amy.

"Come on! They can't go to the police," said Dan. "What will Ian and Evan tell them? That some maniac named Vesper One is planning on blowing up the world and all they have to do is search an entire mountain range to find the hostages and a device that Archimedes made centuries ago? And, by the way, that's why the sky is purple? They'll lock *them* up."

Atticus said, "I think Dan has a point. It would be hard to believe. And by the time the police got up to speed and actually did anything, it might be too late."

Amy considered this and said, "Okay, I'll call in reinforcements." She picked up her phone and punched in the number.

"Hamilton? It's Amy." She quickly explained what had happened. "I need you and Jonah to fly to Washington State right now. You can fly into Seattle and then get to the motel and meet Ian and Evan." She paused, her mouth breaking into a grin. After all the bad news it felt terrific to be able to convey something positive.

"And I've got great news," she said. "Phoenix is alive. And free. He got away from the Vespers. He'll be with Ian and Evan."

"That's awesome, Amy," Hamilton said.

She heard Hamilton say something to Jonah and the international superstar grabbed the phone from Hamilton.

"Amy, is it true? Is Phoenix really safe?"

Amy heard Jonah's fab voice crack and she could almost feel the waves of emotion across the ether.

"He really is, Jonah. You'll be able to see for yourself soon."

She heard a little sob escape from Jonah and he said, "Thanks."

Hamilton came back on the line. "Okay, Amy. We'll be ready to go right away."

"When we're done in DC, we'll fly out there. Phoenix will lead you to the location of the hostages. Do whatever you can to rescue them and stop the Vespers. We'll meet you there as soon as possible."

She clicked off and looked at the others. Dan was watching her with a dark expression.

"It'll be too late, Amy," he said accusingly.

"I don't think so. If Vesper One believes he's won, he'll have a false sense of security. And if we can capture Isabel in DC, we'll have a hostage that we can bargain with. I'm tired of Vesper One holding all the cards."

Dan shook his head stubbornly. "But why would Vesper One give up anything for Isabel? According to you they're probably competing for the top spot of global megalomaniac."

"Because she might have valuable information about Vesper One that he won't want us to learn. And Isabel has resources we don't. If we can force her to work with us, we can employ some of those assets to help us."

"I still think you're wrong," said Dan hotly.

"Fine. Do you want to lead this operation?" Amy said, staring at him.

Under her gaze Dan finally looked down. "I just hope you're right."

"Me, too," Amy said under her breath. "Me, too."

CHAPTER 7

The plane ride was incredibly turbulent and Ian, Evan, and the rest of the passengers on the flight, and maybe even the pilots, probably thought they were actually going to crash. When they approached the airport, the turbulence became so severe that several passengers fainted while others grabbed barf bags and filled them up with their stomach contents. When the plane finally bounced down on the runway and stayed there, everyone cheered.

Ian and Evan looked at each other, their faces pale and their bellies wriggly.

Ian said, "If we survive the Vespers, perhaps we can drive back East. I don't think my stomach can manage another jaunt like that one."

"Yeah," said Evan, holding his stomach. "It must be really windy today. Only reason why it would be so bumpy."

They hustled toward the exit with their bags. When they got outside of the airport they found, to their astonishment, that it was calm and sunny with not even a slight breeze. As they looked around they noticed pilots in their uniforms huddled together talking. Other airline personnel were looking nervous. When Ian looked up into the sky he saw one plane coming in for a landing. It was jerking and whipping all over the place.

He looked at Evan, who had obviously seen this as well.

"What's going on?" Ian asked.

Evan shrugged and quickly walked over to one of the pilots.

"Sir," Evan began. "It's not windy today, but it seems like the planes are having a lot of trouble flying."

The man looked at Evan and said abruptly, "I can't talk about it. Sorry."

He hurriedly moved off.

Evan came back over to Ian. "Nothing we can do about it now. We've got to get to the motel as fast as possible. I don't want to give the Vespers any chance at all to kidnap Phoenix again."

Ian nodded and they both ran toward the cabstand. They quickly found out that it was too far for a cab to take them. But they found a bus that would. They bought tickets and boarded a few minutes before the bus was scheduled to depart.

Both of them were so engrossed in their journey that they failed to see a vehicle that was following them. There were three people inside, but they had hats and glasses on and their coat collars were pulled up, making it impossible to see who they were.

As the bus pulled off, the other vehicle followed closely.

Amy, Dan, and the others climbed into a cab outside of Union Station in DC and headed over to the Smithsonian's National Museum of American History. It was located on the National Mall. The cab dropped them off on Constitution Avenue and they hurried in. Like almost all museums in DC, the admission was free because all of these facilities were paid for largely with tax dollars and thus open to the country's citizens without charge. The space inside was divided up into themes. The first floor focused on transportation and technology. There was a large early-style locomotive anchoring this floor. The second floor housed exhibitions on American lives and ideals, and the National Museum of African American History and Culture Gallery. The third floor focused on wars and politics, and located here was a large exhibition on the men who have been president of the United States.

Amy and the others paused in the large lobby and gazed around.

"Where do we start looking?" asked Dan.

Atticus said, "It makes the most sense to ask someone who works here. Perhaps there's a permanent Lewis and Clark exhibit."

"Good thinking," said Amy. But she added in a

warning tone, "Be on the lookout for Isabel Kabra. And I doubt she'll be traveling alone, so keep watch for her bodyguards, too."

They headed over to the information desk and were told that there was a Lewis and Clark display on the third floor. Meriwether Lewis and William Clark, both veteran soldiers, had been commissioned by President Thomas Jefferson to explore the Northwest Territory that the United States had acquired from France as part of the Louisiana Purchase of 1803. Their journey led them all the way to the Pacific coast. Early on in the trip, Lewis and Clark were joined by a Shoshone Indian named Sacagawea. She helped guide the expedition westward over the Rocky Mountains. It had been the longest, most arduous expedition ever undertaken in America, and both Lewis and Clark became revered as two of the country's greatest heroes.

They took the stairs up to the third floor and quickly found the display area. Items from the legendary expedition were under glass, and there were information cards under every item, explaining what they were and how each had been used by the two famous explorers. However, after twenty minutes of examining all of the items, Amy and the others were no further along in their quest.

Dan said, "If there's something helpful here, I don't see it. I hope this wasn't a huge waste of time. We could have been halfway to the West Coast by now."

Atticus said firmly, "My mother was dying at

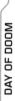

the time. I doubt she would have told me *useless* information."

Dan paled and said, "Hey, Att, I didn't mean it like that. But she could have been delirious."

"No, she wasn't," said Atticus emphatically. "She knew exactly what she was doing. I'm sure of it."

Jake added, "And Isabel Kabra is in town, too."

Amy said, "But we don't know that she actually came here. As you said, DC is a big city. We just speculated it was to look at something pertaining to Lewis and Clark." She added in a hollow voice, "Well, *I* speculated."

While they had been talking, a woman had walked over to them.

"Lot of interest in Lewis and Clark today," said the woman.

They all stared at her. She was tall, around fifty, with brown hair and large brown eyes. She wore a striking red dress and had kindly features.

"You mean other people have been here to see the display?" asked Amy.

"Just a few minutes ago there was someone," said the woman. "I'm Dr. Nancy Gwinn, by the way. I'm one of the curators here. My specialty is Lewis and Clark, actually."

"Then you're just the person we want to see," said Amy.

"Really, why is that?" asked Dr. Gwinn curiously.

Amy said, "We're students traveling here from out of

town. We're doing a team research paper for a regional competition on Lewis and Clark. There are many things that are known about them, of course. But we were hoping to find out some things that aren't so well-known." She pointed to the display cabinet. "We've covered all of these items in our paper, but do you have any *other* artifacts from the expedition?"

Dr. Gwinn nodded. "Yes, we have many that aren't on display. It's a question of space and interest."

"And there seems to be *interest*," said Amy. "Like you said, someone else was in here asking about them. Was that person my age by any chance? A girl about my height? Blond hair, shoulder length? You see, it's a true competition, and there are college scholarships at stake."

Dr. Gwinn shook her head. "No, she was much older. In her forties. Dark hair, attractive. Very intense. In fact, she seemed familiar to me for some reason."

The four looked at each other. That was undoubtedly Isabel Kabra.

"Was she alone?" asked Dan. "That sounds a lot like one of the teachers who's working with the students we're competing against."

"She *was* alone. But now that you say it, she did seem sort of teacherlike in her demeanor. And she was very articulate."

"I'm sure. Did she ask to see anything out of the ordinary?" asked Amy.

Dr. Gwinn thought for a moment. "Well, just one

thing, now that you mention it. The Lewis and Clark compass. She was quite taken with it."

"Compass," said Amy. She snapped her fingers. "That's right. The famous compass." She looked at the others. "We could use that as one of our centerpiece themes for the research paper."

She turned to look at Dr. Gwinn. "Is there any way we can take a look at it, too?"

Dr. Gwinn shook her head. "She had an appointment. It's the Smithsonian's policy not to bring articles from the back of the building without an appointment."

Amy looked crushed. "She told us we didn't need an appointment when I asked her last week. She's also on the competition's organization committee."

"Well, that's hardly fair," said Dr. Gwinn sternly. "It seems that she was trying to deliberately mislead you."

Amy and Dan said nothing but looked at her hopefully.

Dr. Gwinn said, "If she got to see it, I think you should, too. That's only fair. And one of the Smithsonian's most important missions is to educate and enlighten. Give me a few minutes."

After she walked off, Dan said to Amy, "You get better at lying every day. Should I be worried?"

She smiled. "I'm surprised you weren't worried a long time ago. And look who's talking. 'That sounds like a teacher of the students we're competing against'?"

"Hey, I just go with the flow," replied Dan, grinning.

Atticus added, "But now we know that Isabel was here and she was interested in something about Lewis and Clark."

"You were right, Atticus," said Dan. "Good call on your part."

Nancy Gwinn came back holding a black case. She had put on white gloves. She led them over to a table in a corner, set the case down on it, and opened it.

Dr. Gwinn said in an excited tone, "This is the famous compass of Lewis and Clark. It was actually purchased by Meriwether Lewis around 1803 in preparation for the mission that President Thomas Jefferson was sending them on. When the expedition returned to St. Louis in the fall of 1806, very few of the instruments and equipment they had purchased for the trip had survived. Fortunately, this compass was one of them. It was kept by Clark as a souvenir from the journey. Later he presented the compass to a friend of his. His descendants donated it to the Smithsonian in the early 1930s."

She took it out of the black case. "It cost about five dollars back then. Lewis purchased it from a well-known instrument maker, Thomas Whitney. It has a silver-plated brass rim and the box is mahogany. It also has a leather carrying case. It's a very handsome piece."

Amy and the others crowded around for a better look, but none of them could see anything helpful in the object.

On a cue from Amy, Jake and Dan used their cellphone cameras to take shots of the compass.

Amy said, "Can we see the bottom of the box?"

"Funny," said Dr. Gwinn. "That woman asked the very same thing."

She turned it over, and Jake and Dan surreptitiously took photos of it with their phones.

Amy leaned closer to look at the box. She said, "Is that writing on there?"

Dr. Gwinn looked more closely. "Yes. It seems to be a

series of numbers scratched into the surface, although it's been worn down over the years, of course. No one has ever been able to figure out what they mean. It was probably just a notation that either Lewis or Clark made during their journey. And the wooden case made a handy place to do so, I imagine."

Amy glanced at Dan. They both knew that Lewis and Clark had been members of the Tomas branch of the Cahills. The Tomas were known for their stubbornness and the fires in their bellies. They had landed men on the moon, and Lewis and Clark had fought their way to the Pacific coast. Amy doubted that they would have scratched some meaningless numbers into the back of a compass box that William Clark had made sure would survive over the centuries.

Dan said, "Did the woman write the numbers down?"

Dr. Gwinn glanced at him strangely. "Why, yes, she did."

"Thanks so much," said Amy. "You've been a big help."

"In fact, we almost had a disaster," added Dr. Gwinn.

"A disaster?" asked Amy. "What do you mean?"

Dr. Gwinn looked chagrined. "It was my fault, really. I shouldn't have let that woman hold the compass. She dropped it. It bounced under the display case over there. But she was able to get under the table and retrieve it. I checked it over. There was no damage, thank goodness."

Amy and Dan looked at each other but said nothing.

As they turned to leave Dr. Gwinn said, "You all were a lot nicer than she was. I hope you win your competition."

Amy and Dan turned back and together said, "Me, too."

CHAPTER 8

Talking the whole time, the four excitedly left the museum.

Jake and Dan showed the others the pictures they'd taken of the compass, front and back.

"Can you enlarge your image so we get a better look?" Amy asked Jake.

He nodded and did so. They fixed their gazes on the photos and kept commenting on various ideas and theories as they walked along.

So preoccupied were they with this that they didn't see the four black SUVs screech to a stop on the street next to them until it was almost too late.

The doors opened and men poured out.

One leaped at Amy, but the six-foot-two-inch Jake leveled him with a textbook football tackle. The man flew backward and crashed into two other men climbing out of one of the SUVs.

Amy shouted, "Scramble, now!"

"Go, Att, go!" yelled Jake at his little brother.

The four ran off in different directions. This was a maneuver that Amy had had them practice for a long time. Four different directions meant that their pursuers would have to split up, too. And it increased the odds that at least one of them would escape.

As Amy sprinted away she glanced across the street and saw Isabel staring at her with unconcealed hatred. When Isabel saw that Amy had spotted her, she turned and ran off down an alley.

Amy quickly formed a plan and slowed down to let the two men chasing her catch up. Amy had trained hard to become a world-class fighter. But even with all that work she still had doubts about her combat abilities. Even now she could feel the nerves building inside her. But she didn't have time to be nervous or doubtful. So she just let her training take over.

When the men were about to grab her, Amy executed a spinning kick right to the first man's knee. Her blow bent it backward and the man screamed and went down to the pavement. Amy knew that when you took out the knee, you took the fight right out of an opponent for two reasons. First, he couldn't stand anymore. And second, it hurt him too much to think about fighting.

The second man slowed and started to pull his gun. Amy never let him get there. She went low, supporting herself on one arm, pivoted, and hit the man with a whip kick, lifting his feet from under him. He crashed back on the pavement. Before he could begin to rise, Amy finished him off with two hard elbow strikes to the jaw.

Then she was up and running hard after Isabel. The woman was not going to get away this time. She was probably the only leverage they would ever have over Vesper One. Amy flew down the alley.

There was no way the older woman could outrun her. Amy could sprint like a gazelle. She was thinking, too, that despite what Ted's Morse code had implied and what they had learned previously, Isabel might very well be Vesper One. If she was, they could use her to turn the tide and wreck the Vespers' plans to destroy the world. At the very least they could find out why Isabel was so interested in the compass.

Amy started to slow down as the alley grew narrower, darker, and definitely more sinister. It was like day had turned into night here. She stopped when she rounded a corner and found that the alley was a dead end. She was staring up at a brick wall that was six stories high.

But what had happened to Isabel? There was no door, window, or fire escape. Nothing.

But, no, there was something.

A big blue dumpster.

Amy assumed her favorite martial arts fighting stance. She took a few steps forward. She was confident that she could kick Isabel's butt, but Amy had to admit that Isabel terrified her. After all, this was the woman who had burned Amy's parents up in a house and had very nearly killed her and Dan a slew of times. Even now she could feel the cold dread spiking up her spine. And her mouth was so dry it was like someone had stuffed it full of cotton balls.

But now was not the time for her courage to fail. She had to keep her wits about her. Amy knew she would have to be wary of poisons, a staple of the Lucian branch. Isabel might have a hidden needle in a ring, or perhaps embedded in her shoe. Whatever the case, Amy would be ready. This was one-on-one. And she was going to take Isabel down, finally. She balled up her courage and prepared to face one of her worst nightmares: Isabel Kabra.

"I know you're here, Isabel, so you might as well just come out now."

Amy didn't think her words would have any effect on the woman, so she was surprised when Isabel Kabra stepped out from behind the dumpster and held her arms up.

"I guess you've won this round, Amy Cahill," snarled Isabel. "But the plan will go on, even without me."

"I don't think so, Isabel," Amy said, looking at her cautiously. She didn't trust Isabel as far as she could throw her, which was not very far at all. "We're going to use you to destroy the Doomsday device Archimedes designed."

"So you know about that, do you?"

"No, but now I have confirmation of it, thanks bunches."

Isabel looked furious at having given this key element away, but then her malicious smile returned. "You can't win, you know."

"I was about to tell you the same thing."

"We seem to have a standoff."

Amy pulled a pair of zip cuffs from her pocket. She had brought these with her for just this sort of situation. "Not really. Get down on your knees, hands behind your head, fingers interlocked."

"And if I don't?"

"If you don't, you'll be very sorry. And your perfect hair will no longer be perfect. That's a promise."

"You didn't think I was going to actually fight you myself, did you?"

"I don't see anybody else here."

Isabel clapped her hands. The dumpster opened and three large men climbed out and quickly encircled Amy.

Amy froze, her limbs quivering with fear. This had been a trap all along. And she'd fallen right into it like an idiot.

"Say good-bye to your life, Amy Cahill," gloated Isabel. "I'm sure there will be a few people who will miss you, misguided though they are."

Amy eyed Isabel. "We know you're not Vesper One. You're not smart enough. And you're predictable. The

Vespers never would have elected you as their leader. You're strictly the B-Team."

Isabel glared darkly at her but said nothing.

"You're too into your stupid fake charities. They needed someone with real vision."

"I have vision," declared Isabel heatedly. "I have more vision than anyone."

"You've got nothing. Even your kids wised up and realized you're an idiot. An evil one, but still an idiot."

"The world will find out how smart I am," shouted Isabel.

"The only way to do that is for you to become Vesper One. And that will never happen."

Amy watched Isabel closely. She could almost see the wheels spinning inside the woman's head.

"Well, unfortunately, Amy, you will not be around to see my triumph." She nodded at her men. "Kill her. Now."

The men drew closer. They did not assume fighting stances. They merely pulled their guns out, which had suppressors attached to the muzzles, and pointed them at Amy's head.

Amy took a deep breath as she stared at the Sig Sauer 9mm pointed at her.

I'm sorry, Dan. But you've got to keep going. You've got to stop them. You've got to.

Amy closed her eyes and prepared to die.

Just at that moment, they all heard it.

Sirens erupting all over the place. They heard cars

squealing down the alley, sirens blasting. They heard doors opening and then slamming closed. Rushing feet, voices calling out tactical orders. The crackle of walkie-talkies. The sounds of gun slides being racked back. And then the thudding sounds of a helicopter in the sky. A PA system blared out: "This is the police. Put your weapons down now and come out with your hands up. There is no escape."

Isabel screamed at her men, "Get me out of here now!"

The men quickly pushed aside the dumpster, revealing a manhole cover. While her men covered Amy and the oncoming cops with their guns, Isabel slipped down into the hole. Her men quickly followed. The last one slid the heavy cover back into place with a clang.

Amy rushed forward and tried to lift the cover but she wasn't strong enough. She turned back to the sounds of the cops, which had grown ever closer. She quickly thought about what she would say to them.

Then Dan poked his head around the corner.

Amy looked at him, stunned.

"Dan?" She looked behind him. "Where are the cops?"

He held up his phone. "I doubled back and saw what was happening. I downloaded an action movie onto my phone and played the scene where the SWAT team comes in to save the day. With my amp upgrade and movie-quality, modified speakers on steroids, it sounded like the real thing, didn't it?"

She smiled. "Yeah, it did. You're a freaking genius."

She walked over to him and squeezed him tight.

"I love you, little brother. And thanks for saving my life."

The two stood there for a long moment just holding on to each other. Tears slid down Amy's face because she knew how close she had come to never seeing her brother again.

And tears slid down Dan's face because he realized the very same thing.

CHAPTER 9

The bus pulled to a stop outside the motel. It was designed to look like a Swiss ski chalet, although there was no snow and thus no skiers. Ian and Evan stepped off the bus, the only passengers to disembark here. The bus pulled off and they stood there looking around.

Ian said, "This truly is the middle of nowhere."

"No, where they've got the hostages is the middle of nowhere," Evan pointed out. "To them this would be paradise."

Ian looked at him guiltily, no doubt thinking of his sister. "You're right. Let's go find Phoenix."

As it turned out they didn't have to. Phoenix found *them*.

Before they even reached the front door of the motel, Phoenix rushed over to them from a shadowy corner.

"I've been watching for you," he explained.

Evan was startled when Phoenix hugged him so tightly that he thought his already queasy stomach might give back whatever was in it. But he also realized that Phoenix was just a kid and had just been through an ordeal that would have paralyzed most adults.

Both Evan and Ian noted that Phoenix was dirty and thin and looked like he hadn't eaten in weeks.

"It's okay; you're not alone anymore," said Evan, patting him on the back.

"Quite right," added Ian. "The light cavalry is in position and we'll be calling up reinforcements in no time. It's time to snatch victory from the jaws of defeat."

Evan said, "Phoenix, are you hurt?"

"Just bumps and bruises and some cuts from when I fell. And from crawling around the countryside. The mountains have lots of sharp edges."

Evan, once more noting Phoenix's emaciated look, said, "Let's get you something to eat. You can tell us everything then. Okay?"

Ian added, "Right. A bit of food and you'll feel so much better."

Phoenix looked torn. He was indeed hungry, but he was obviously also thinking about the other hostages. Finally, his belly won out.

"Okay, but let's hurry."

They walked into a small restaurant just off the lobby and sat down at a table.

Outside, the vehicle was mostly hidden behind a large tree but still had a clear view of the motel's front entrance. Sandy Bancroft, the intrepid weatherman and also Vesper Four, was driving. In the front passenger seat was the malicious and highly danger-ous Cheyenne Wyoming, also known as Vesper Six.

"So that's where our little one got to," commented Sandy.

"Stunned that he was able to escape," groused Cheyenne, looking accusingly at Sandy.

"My dear girl, these things happen. But we have now reacquired the wayward youth and we can exe-cute our plan. In fact, it's much better now."

"I guess I see that."

"Two additional hostages. As Vesper *Six* I would very much hope that you *would* see that."

Cheyenne cast him a dirty look. "Don't push it, Vesper *Four*. No one died and made you supreme being."

"True, so very true. We all know who our leader is, don't we, Cheyenne?"

He glanced at her with a gleeful condescension. She merely looked away.

"How do you want to do this?" she asked.

"The plan is set," Sandy said sharply. "Just *execute* the plan. No deviations, my dear. None!" He did not sound the least bit nice or charming now.

A sullen Cheyenne climbed out of the vehicle and walked off to "execute" the plan.

Inside the restaurant, Phoenix had just finished telling Ian and Evan everything he knew.

Evan said, "Okay, that's very helpful. Now let's fill you in from our end."

Evan and Ian took turns telling Phoenix all that had happened while he had been a hostage.

Evan said, "We haven't heard back from Amy and the others yet. But I e-mailed them about hearing from you. They know we're out here. I'm sure they'll be here soon."

Ian studied Phoenix. "You're sure that the hostages are okay? And *Natalie*?"

"Everyone is sort of like me. Hungry, dirty, dinged up, but okay. Well, Nellie got shot. But she's okay, too."

Evan's phone buzzed. He looked at the long text, his eyes widening as he did so.

"Amy and the others were attacked in DC by Isabel and her goons. They barely got out alive."

Ian groaned. "God, I hate my mother. What happened?"

Evan read over the text once more and explained why the others were in DC.

"They went there when we told them Isabel was on her way to Washington," he added.

"But Lewis and Clark's compass?" Ian said curiously. "My mother was interested in that? Why?"

"Amy doesn't say. She also says that they think Riley McGrath is Vesper One, but that's not his real name."

"Well, we know that," said Ian. "We found out about him when we hacked Sinead's e-mails. Riley McGrath was a park ranger. And he's dead. Vesper One just assumed his identity. Doesn't really help us much. He probably has lots of identities."

"She also said that Hamilton and Jonah are on their way here. We're to wait and meet them."

"Jonah is coming?" said Phoenix. He idolized his famous cousin, though he didn't think much of his songwriting abilities. In that, he wasn't alone. Many people, while acknowledging that Jonah had a great voice, didn't like his songs. But millions of others did, so he was a superstar. It was just how the world worked.

"Yes. And they might get here faster than we did. Jonah has his own plane."

"We have to hurry," said Phoenix. "Right now all the hostages are okay, but that might change."

They both looked at him.

Evan said slowly, "Uh, Phoenix, I guess you don't know."

"Know what?"

Evan looked at Ian, who said quietly, "Alistair is dead, Phoenix. I'm sorry."

Phoenix looked at both of them, small clusters of tears gathering in his eyes. "Alistair's dead?" He looked like he might start sobbing. "But he was okay the last time I saw him."

"I'm sure he was," said Ian. "I'm sorry to have to be the one to tell you."

"He might have just given up," said Evan quietly. "Sometimes people do."

Phoenix covered his face with his hands and wept

softly. Evan looked nervously around the restaurant to see if anyone was watching, but luckily no one was. He dipped a napkin in his glass of water and gave it to Phoenix to wipe his face.

"I know it's hard, Phoenix. But we have to keep moving on, to help the other hostages."

Ian was about to say something else when he looked up and said, "That was extraordinarily fast."

The others turned and saw Hamilton and Jonah rush in, spot them, and head their way.

They all hugged one another and shook hands. Phoenix gave Jonah a particularly hard squeeze and the international superstar hugged him back just as tightly.

"Good to see you, big guy," said Jonah.

"Yeah," said Phoenix happily, the tears still shiny on his face.

"How'd you get here so fast?" asked Ian.

"Private wings," said Hamilton. "It's definitely something I could get used to."

"Was it really bumpy?" asked Evan.

Jonah said, "Yeah. I thought we were going to crash a couple of times. I asked the pilot about it. He said his instruments went nuts. He finally had to fly and then land the plane manually, and even then he said it was a nightmare."

They all sat and Evan filled them in on what they knew.

"Aren't you Jonah Wizard?"

They all looked up at the tall, plump, middle-aged waitress who stood in front of them.

Jonah inwardly groaned as she gazed at him in adoration. But he smiled and said convincingly, "Actually, I get that a lot. But I'm not Jonah Wizard. Can't even carry a tune."

"Really?" she said, though her tone was not disappointed. "I think you are Jonah Wizard." She turned to the others. "And you're Evan and Ian and Hamilton and of course poor little Phoenix."

They all stared up at her in astonishment.

She pulled aside her apron, revealing a gun in her right hand.

"And that's a Cobra .45 semiautomatic chambered with wicked Silvertip ordnance that will blow very large holes in all of you. So unless you want extra perforations in your heads, I suggest you quietly follow me outside. Now!"

The boys stood and walked outside with the waitress trailing them.

There was a van parked there. In the driver's seat was Casper Wyoming. Sandy was in the passenger seat.

"Excellent work, Cheyenne," he said.

"Cheyenne!" exclaimed Ian as he glanced back at her.

She whipped off her wig, popped out colored contact lenses, and spit out cotton balls from her mouth. "A little body padding to add twenty pounds, face putty to make wrinkles, and voilà, even someone beautiful can be made to look ugly," she said.

"You are ugly," shot back Phoenix. "On the *inside*."

She grabbed his collar and threw him in the van.

She pointed her gun at the others. "Get in. Now!"

They all climbed in and Cheyenne shut the door. The van's windows were tinted so no one could see them. Casper drove off, while Sandy covered the others with his gun. Cheyenne used zip cuffs to bind the guys' hands. Then she put hoods over their heads so they couldn't see where they were going.

"Excellent," said Sandy. "I'm impressed with how well our little operation went. But then again, the opposition was particularly amateurish and thus underwhelming." He looked at Ian. "You know, Ian, your mother would be so disappointed that you turned against the Kabra family."

"She's not part of our family. Not anymore," snapped Ian.

"Excellent," said Sandy again. "It's so much easier to kill non-family members."

CHAPTER 10

By prearrangement Amy and Dan met up with Jake and Atticus at the hotel in DC where they were staying. When Amy told Jake and Atticus how she had nearly died, Jake paled, rose from his seat, and put his arms around her.

"Ames, that was way too close."

"I'd be dead if it weren't for my supersmart little brother," said Amy, gazing at Dan, but hugging Jake.

Jake released Amy and shook Dan's hand. "We all owe you big for that one, Dan."

"Hey, she's my sister. She doesn't get to leave me by myself. I've got years left to make her life miserable."

Amy could tell that Dan was saying this just to lighten the moment, to put firmly in the past how close he'd come to losing her. Well, she thought, he was mostly doing it for that. Little brothers were little brothers, after all. And at times he certainly did make her life miserable. But he had also just saved it. So he could make her as miserable as he wanted.

Amy looked at Jake. "How did you guys get away?"

"Those dudes were big but slow," said Jake. "They ran out of gas after half a mile. Some bad guys. Isabel needs to hire fitter criminals."

Amy sat down. "Okay, I texted Evan what happened to us in DC and about Riley McGrath possibly being Vesper One. Hopefully, they've reached Phoenix by now. But we need to move on fast. Jake, let's see the pictures you took of the compass again."

Jake pulled out his phone and brought the photos up.

"Can you enlarge them?" asked Amy.

"Coming up," replied Jake. He hit some keys and the pictures swelled.

Dan eyed one photo and said, "I don't see anything remarkable. It just looks like an old compass."

He brought up the photos he'd taken and stared at them one after another. "Nothing."

"Isabel would not have come all this way just to look at an old compass," said Amy. "There has to be something. Let's see the back."

Jake hit another key and the next photo came up on the screen. It was the back of the compass box.

Amy said, "Okay, there are the numbers. The ones that Dr. Gwinn said no one had figured out."

"Right," said Atticus. "Maybe there's something there. My mother obviously wanted us to find out about this compass."

"Can you make them larger?" Amy asked Jake.

He made the numbers as big as possible.

They all stared at them.

Amy said, "Okay, that looks to be a four and a seven."

"And the letter *M* or *N*," added Dan.

Atticus squinted. "That's a twelve," he said, pointing to a number just below the four and seven. "At least I think so."

Dan said, "And a number one after it. So one twenty-one."

Amy said, "I think so. And there's a letter behind the one twenty-one. Looks to be a *W.*"

Atticus said, "Okay, to recap we have forty-seven and the letter *M* or *N.* And a one-two-one with a minus sign. And the letter *W.* What does that tell us?"

He looked at the others. Jake shrugged. Amy looked uncertain.

Dan, however, was on his laptop. "When in doubt, let's go to the web," he muttered.

He put in the information they had and hit the SEARCH key.

He looked up, smiling sarcastically. "Only one

billion, nine hundred and sixty-three million, four hundred and seventy-nine thousand, eight hundred and sixteen possibilities. I should be able to get through them in the next seven thousand, eight hundred and fourteen years. Just sit tight and call up lots of room service."

Atticus suddenly looked excited. "Dan, search for the *map* coordinates of the Cascade Mountain Range."

Amy said, "Why the—" She blinked. "Right, I get it; Dan, quick, do it."

Dan was already punching the keys on his laptop. It took only a few seconds.

He looked up this time in genuine triumph. "Forty-seven degrees north latitude and one hundred twenty-one degrees west longitude is the exact location of the Cascade Mountain Range. So the letter was an *N* for *north*, and not an *M*!"

Atticus added, "That confirms what we learned from Phoenix. That must be where the hostages are."

"And the Cascades have a massive subduction zone," added Jake. "We already knew that. Perfect for the Vespers' Doomsday device."

Dan said, "See, Amy, we should've just gone directly there without wasting time in DC."

Amy replied, "No, we've now *confirmed* what Phoenix told us. And even though I nearly died, it was worth it to see the look on Isabel's face when I told her she would never be Vesper One."

"You must have really made her mad," said Dan.

"Oh, I did. But that's not the only reason I did it. But forget her. We need to get to the West Coast as fast as possible. We'll hook up with the others, save the hostages, and destroy the Doomsday device."

"And nail the Vespers," Dan reminded her.

"Never fear, little brother, I would never forget that important detail."

Atticus looked confused. "But why would Isabel have gone to DC to figure out where the hostages and the Doomsday device are? Wouldn't she already know?"

"Not if Vesper One is keeping things from her," said Amy with a smile. "And that might just work out to our advantage." She looked at Dan. "Call the airline and get us tickets on the next flight out to Washington State."

Dan got on the phone with his credit card ready. But the lines were jammed. He couldn't get through. He tried ten times with five different airlines. He slammed the phone down in frustration.

Meanwhile, Jake had turned on the TV in the room. After a minute of watching a late-breaking news story he said, "Amy, I think I know why we can't get through to the airlines. Look."

Amy turned to stare at the screen. After a few seconds seeing what was unfolding all over the country, her spirits sank. They weren't going to be able to get to the West Coast after all.

At least not via plane.

CHAPTER 11

Staring at the TV screen, Amy learned that all air traffic in the world had been grounded because of a number of near-crashes. The mishaps had been because of failure of the planes' avionics systems. Since it was inconceivable that all of the planes' avionics would fail on the same day, the authorities had checked for other causes. They had quickly determined that changes in the magnetic fields of the Earth had taken place. And those changes were causing potentially catastrophic interference with pilots' ability to control their aircraft, which depended on stable magnetic fields.

Dan looked at Amy. Amy looked at Dan. Atticus and Jake stared at them both.

Dan said, "Are you thinking what I'm thinking?"

Amy slowly nodded. "A change in the Earth's magnetic fields. That means there must have been some significant disruption in the magnetic poles. That could only mean . . ." Her voice trailed off.

Dan swallowed with difficulty. "Either aliens are about to eat us, or the Vespers have already begun to activate their Doomsday device."

Atticus said calmly, "Since the Earth is still here I think the key phrase is 'begun to activate.' If they had triggered it fully, we would see far more catastrophic results."

"Oh, goody," snapped Dan. "I can't wait for the far more catastrophic results."

"Att means we still have a shot at stopping things," said Jake. "Remember Vesper One got the gear and other stuff in New York. He had to get out to the West Coast and put it together in the device. That takes time."

"Time we're obviously running out of," said Amy. "Like Atticus said, the activation process has begun. Planes were flying just fine earlier. I saw them in the sky."

"But we still might have a shot," said Jake.

"Oh, really?" said Amy. "How? How do we get out to the West Coast and stop them if we can't fly? You want us to ride a bike? Take a cab? Board a FREAKING bus? It'll take forever. Vesper One already sent us that link with the hostages. He's planning to kill them. He probably already *has* killed them. What's to stop him?"

Atticus pushed his glasses farther up his nose from where they had slid down and said, "I think he wants us to be there when it happens."

"What?" said Amy.

"I THINK HE WANTS US TO BE THERE WHEN IT HAPPENS," shouted Atticus.

"I *heard* you," said Amy. "I just don't *understand* you."

"Vesper One is highly intelligent, determined, and forceful," stated Atticus.

"He's also ruthless, murderous, and he probably has really bad BO," shot back Dan.

"Granted," said Atticus. "But he's also highly competitive, even megalomaniacal, like most of the Vespers. He's been giving us clues and hints and tidbits of his plans throughout this whole ordeal. He's been using us, essentially, to get what he needed to build the Doomsday device."

"And he succeeded," snapped Dan. "We got him everything he needed. He built it. He's pulled the trigger on it. He doesn't need us or the hostages anymore."

"But now, right as he's about to perform the final act on his little world-destruction plan, the only thing missing is *us*. His opponents in all this. He needs us as part of the final act. So he can not only rub our noses in it but kill us at the same time. It's just what the Vespers do."

"I still don't think—" began Amy.

"He didn't need to send us that link with the hostages, Amy," interrupted Atticus. "He'd already won, or so he thinks. So why did he?"

"Just his way of, like you said, rubbing our noses in it."

"It was a link, Amy. It wasn't a real-time transmission. Which means that Vesper One had time to look at it before it went out to us. Now, I recognized pretty much right away that Ted was using his blinking as Morse code to convey information to us. Do you really think Vesper One, as smart as he is, failed to see that, too? But he still let the link go out. So I'm thinking that the initial activation of the device was done to alert us that time was running out. Of course Vesper One's ego won't let him even consider the possibility that if we do get there, we'll be smart enough to beat him. But make no mistake, he wants us there."

They all stood there looking stunned by this theory.

Atticus added, "And also keep in mind that no one alive has actually seen what the Doomsday device Archimedes designed can do. Vesper One thinks he's figured it out, but even he will have to exercise some degree of caution. It will take him some time to test it."

Dan said, "You know, Amy, what Atticus is saying actually makes sense."

Amy slowly nodded. "I'm starting to think the same thing. So if he's waiting for us to appear—"

Jake finished for her, "—then that might give us the one chance we need to beat him."

"But how do we get to the West Coast?" said Amy.

Dan had continued working on his laptop while they were discussing things. "The train," he announced.

"The train?" exclaimed Amy. "You can take a *train* across the country?"

"Actually, it requires two trains. The Capitol Limited from right here in DC. It goes to Chicago. Leaves this afternoon at five and gets into Chicago tomorrow morning. Then we take a second train from Chicago to Seattle. That takes forty-six hours."

"Forty-six hours!" cried out Amy.

"In the interest of full disclosure it's actually forty-six hours and ten minutes," amended Dan.

"I can fly around the world in forty-six hours and ten minutes," barked Amy.

"The operative word being *fly*," said Atticus.

Dan looked at his sister. "What other option do we have?"

Her face took on a resolute look. "Buy the tickets, Dan." She looked at her watch. "We'll have just enough time to catch this Capitol Limited train thingy."

While Dan did that and Jake and Atticus were getting their stuff ready, Amy texted Evan. It bounced back. She tried to call him. It went to voice mail. She tried to contact Jonah, Hamilton, and Ian. The same result. She wondered if the magnetic pole disruption also had affected wireless communications on the ground. As a test, she texted Dan. He looked up from his computer when the text landed in his mailbox and his phone chirped.

"Why are you texting me? I'm right here."

Amy didn't answer. Now she knew something was very wrong.

CHAPTER 12

It was a tight fit.

Jonah, Hamilton, Ian, Evan, and Phoenix were tied up in a small, darkened room. They were each trying to figure out where they were.

Evan had counted off the seconds in his head on the drive, and gauging the speed of the van he figured they were about two hours and a hundred miles away from the motel. However, he couldn't tell in which direction. If south, they would be near Seattle or Tacoma. If north, they could be in Canada.

He told this to the others.

"Or east and west," Ian pointed out.

"No," said Evan. "Two hours west and we're in the ocean. And why go east? The subduction zone is along the coast."

Jonah perked up and asked the others if they wanted him to sing to keep their spirits up. "Be glad to do it, bros," he added with a dazzling smile.

The immediate consensus was that none of their spirits had reached such a level of depression that warranted Jonah's musical intervention.

"Well, just let me know when it does," Jonah said, attempting to sound cheerful.

"How about never?" Hamilton mumbled under his breath.

Phoenix said, "I wonder if they're going to take us to the other hostages."

Ian piped in, "Let's hope no more of them are dead." He closed his eyes and a small tear appeared at the edge of his right eyelid.

A noise made them all fall silent.

A door opened and a light appeared through the opening. It was just a narrow shaft of illumination. They heard footsteps growing closer. It was still too dark for them to see who it was.

Ian stiffened and opened his eyes when he felt something press against the back of his head.

It was the muzzle of a Glock pistol with a suppressor can attached.

Casper Wyoming's voice came out of the darkness. "Get up, Kabra. Someone very special wants to see you."

"Who?" exclaimed Ian. "My sister?"

"I said special, not stupid. Like *you*."

Casper jerked Ian up, lifting him completely off the ground. But when Ian came down he made certain that he landed on top of Casper's foot. Hard.

"Oww!" yelped Casper.

"So sorry," said Ian, trying to hide his grin. "But

after all, as you so helpfully pointed out, I am quite stupid."

"Maybe I'll shoot you right here," growled Casper, putting the gun muzzle against Ian's head again.

"I don't believe you can," said Ian.

"Oh, yeah? Why's that?"

"As you said, someone very special wants to see me. I'm sure you don't want to disappoint the person."

Hamilton added, "Yeah, you might get in trouble, doofus."

Casper eyed him grimly. "Just give me a reason, Holt. Just one reason."

"If you untie me, I'll give you ten of them wrapped around my fists. They'll be the last things you ever see."

"You don't scare me, muscle man."

"Sure I do. And my time will come."

Ian snapped, "Let's get a move on. You don't want to keep your fearless leader waiting."

"Hey, I'm giving the orders around here, not you," barked Casper.

"All right. So what action do you propose we take?" Ian stared up at him expectantly.

Casper hesitated, his mind evidently trying to think of something pithy to come back with. But failing that, he simply said, "Let's get a move on."

"Right," said Ian, smiling triumphantly. "Bloody well wish I'd thought of that."

"Doofus," muttered Hamilton, staring at Casper.

Casper pushed Ian forward, slamming the door and locking it behind him.

Casper led Ian into another room. He turned on a light and Ian blinked to adjust to the brightness. He saw that there was a large TV screen on one wall. Casper hit a button on a console and the screen crackled to life.

At first the screen remained black, but then someone appeared there. Ian took an involuntary step back, and shuddered.

His mother, Isabel Kabra, was staring at him.

Could she see him? Ian wondered. Then he noticed the TV camera bolted to the wall. It was pointing at him.

As if in answer to his unspoken question, his mother snapped, "Of course I can see you."

"What do you want?" retorted Ian.

"You have betrayed me. You have turned against your own family."

"No, you're the one that turned against *us*," Ian said hotly.

She ignored this. "However, being of a kind and compassionate nature—"

Ian snorted at this remark, but she ignored this, too, and continued. "The only reason you're not dead is because, in keeping with my compassionate nature, I have decided to give you a second chance."

"Why?" he shot back.

"I'm a loving, caring mother and, therefore, I don't want to have to kill my own son."

Ian scowled. "I don't believe anything you say."

"I'm on my way out to see you, son. And your sister, Natalie. If you're smart, and I hope you are, you will reconsider your loyalties and side with me. If you continue to support the Cahills, only death awaits you. *And* your sister. It will be out of my hands. It really will be."

"You don't care what happens to us. You bloody well shot your own daughter!"

"It was just a flesh wound. To my knowledge, no one has ever died from being shot in the foot. Perhaps a permanent limp, a bit of arthritis, but is that really so bad?"

"You're barking mad. You could've *killed* her."

"On the contrary, did you know that certain of the Vespers *did* want to kill your sister? I intervened and they shot Nellie Gomez instead. Worse the luck she survived. Why aim for the shoulder when a perfectly good head was right there? I will never understand. However, the fact remains: But for me, your precious sister would be dead. So, you see, dear boy, I *do* care."

"They should have kept you in prison. You simply bought your way out. It's pathetic."

Isabel took a step closer, nearly filling the screen. The charm bracelet she never took off rattled on her wrist. "I raised you to be a Lucian. I raised you to be loyal." She paused and added quietly, "I suppose I should tell you."

"Tell me what?"

"I'm dying."

Ian snorted. "Right. Do you think I'm a fool?"

She held up her arm and let her sleeve slide down. There was a large reddish-purple mass on it.

"Poisoned, Ian. Slow-acting, but irreversible. From the South American blowfish. My death will not be pretty."

Ian stared at the disfigured arm. It looked quite painful, but he knew his mother too well to be fooled. "How could someone poison you? You're the queen of poisoners. You poison others, not the other way around."

"I went to visit your father, Vikram."

"What? Why?" Ian hadn't seen his father in quite some time. Not since Vikram had fled the country for South America after abandoning his family.

"He's my husband. I love him. I've always loved him. He had fallen ill. Nothing life threatening, but he was in the hospital. But it was really a trap set by my enemies. Instead of seeing your father I got this, administered by a kindly old woman dressed as a nurse who I took to be totally harmless until she stuck the needle into my arm." She paused. "I calculate that I have at most five days to live." She lowered her arm and her sleeve slid back down. "The organ shutdown will be massive and linear. Death will follow almost immediately."

"I . . . I don't believe you."

"I completely understand why you feel that way, son."

This response surprised Ian. He had always assumed that his mother would never understand how another person felt about anything.

She said, "But the fact is, as one grows close to death, the only thing that matters is family, Ian. I hope you can see that."

Isabel's tone had lost its aggressiveness. It was lower, gentler. Her features had softened, too. She was a very attractive woman when she wasn't running around as a homicidal maniac killing people and shouting things like, "Everyone must die. Now!"

Ian stared into his mother's big eyes.

"But if you saved Natalie, then you were behind her kidnapping. It's the only way you could have known where she was."

"That's not so, Ian. I wasn't behind it. Someone else was. When I found out I took the steps necessary to see that my children were not hurt."

"When I called and told you Natalie had been taken, you said you didn't have *any* children."

"Because that's how I felt back then, son. I felt abandoned. By you and your sister. You must forgive an unfortunate choice of words."

"So what's changed, then?"

She held up her damaged arm once more. "This. *This* has changed. This makes a person stop and think. Reprioritize. I'm not immortal, Ian. I'm nearly fifty, even though I barely look thirty. But I don't have all that much time left. I want to make the most of it."

She drew a deep breath and focused those large, soft eyes on her son.

"I want my family, what's left of it, back, Ian. I want my children back. With their mother, where they belong."

Ian was sniffling now. "How do I know I can trust you?"

"How can anyone know that about anyone? But you *are* a Lucian. You can't deny that. You competed mightily against Amy and Dan and the others, and you did well. Very well. It was your true nature. And being Lucians, our natural home is with the Vespers. It's how we're wired. We're not tree huggers. We're not for the greater good. We're for the greater *us*. But now here you are, working *with* them. And against your family. How can that be, son? You are going against everything you believe in. Indeed, I'm the one who should be asking how I can trust *you*."

Ian broke down crying. "I'm . . . I'm sorry, Mother. I'm sorry."

"It's all right, baby. Mother knows." Her voice was silky smooth, comforting. "Don't cry, my sweet boy. It will be all right. Mother will make it all right."

Ian wiped his eyes. "What do you want me to do?"

"You have to prove your loyalty to me, Ian. It is imperative in my final days on earth."

"How?"

"It will not be easy. But the important things in life never are."

"What is it?"

"I want you to kill one of the hostages. Not your sister, of course. But any of the others will do. If you execute that order, I will welcome you and your sister back into the family with open arms for the time I have left."

"Do I really have to?" he wailed. "I mean, kill someone?"

"Yes, darling, you really do," she cooed back. "But it won't be that hard. Just think like a Lucian. It'll come naturally. We're very good at killing. It's not actually that difficult. You just have to really want to."

"And if I don't?"

"The consequences will be severe, Ian. For you and your sister. I hope I've made myself clear. I love you both, but I've worked too hard to let my grand plan slip away."

"Can I ask a favor first?" said Ian timidly.

Isabel's face hardened but almost immediately relaxed once more. "Certainly, sweetheart. Ask away."

"I'd like to see Natalie. I've really missed her."

"Of course, baby. Of course you can see her. You're right. You've been separated for far too long. You'll see her right now."

"Thanks, Mom."

She blew him a little kiss. "I'll see you soon, darling."

On a cue from Isabel, Casper led Ian away.

A figure came out of the shadows. It was Cheyenne. She looked at Isabel, who was still up on the screen.

Cheyenne said, "I hope you're not getting weak."

"Meaning what precisely?" snapped Isabel.

"You told Ian not to kill his sister."

"Oh, that?" Isabel laughed. "That was rather selfish on my part."

"Yeah, I get that. She's your daughter."

Isabel's features turned ice-cold. "I have no daughter. I didn't want Ian to kill her because if he fails to do what I have instructed, I want the pleasure of killing them *both*. Personally. Now why don't you go do something useful, like maim someone? Oh, and tell that thickheaded brother of yours that if he screws up again like he did in Switzerland, there won't be enough left of him to put in a tablespoon."

"Sorry to hear about your being poisoned," Cheyenne said snidely.

Isabel smiled imperiously. "You didn't really believe that rubbish, did you?" She held up her arm, revealing the ugly mass. She rubbed at it with a cloth she took from her pocket. The colors from the mass came off on the cloth.

"Works great for Halloween parties, too," she said icily.

"You are one cold woman."

"Well, cold beats warmth every time. And don't ever forget it."

The screen went black.

CHAPTER 13

The Chicago Limited train pulled out of Union Station in Washington, DC, with a long groan of metal wheels on metal rails. The train was packed because, ironically enough in the twenty-first century, with all flights grounded, the train was proving the only real option left to cover exceptionally long distances. Few people wanted to spend a solid week driving themselves across the country. Indeed, Amtrak had added more cars to allow for the sudden demand to ride the rails instead of the not-so-friendly skies.

Dan and Amy were sharing one sleeper compartment while Jake and Atticus were rooming together in another. Dan sat glumly in his little seat, staring out the window. He checked his cell phone. Reception was spotty. He keyed his laptop, tried to get on the Internet. He succeeded, and then when they went through a tunnel, he lost the connection. He sighed and looked at Amy.

"This sucks," he said.

"What does?"

"I feel like I'm back in the nineteenth century. What do we take after the train, a stagecoach?"

"It is what it is, Dan," replied Amy. "And need I remind you that the train was *your* idea?"

"That doesn't mean I have to like it."

Amy looked back down at the book she was reading.

"Is that chick lit?" asked Dan sullenly.

"And what if it is?" she shot back.

"The world is about to end and you're reading about guys and girls and sappy love stories?"

She held up the book. "It's actually a book on sub-duction zones and their geological makeup. I found it in the science section of the train station bookstore. So no sappy love stories required."

Dan's face flushed and he looked away. "Good, okay, just checking."

Amy shook her head and went back to reading.

Dan's cell phone vibrated. When he looked down his heart nearly stopped. He quickly glanced up to see if his sister had heard the vibration, but she still was reading her book.

Dan quietly picked up the phone and read the text that had just dropped in his mailbox. It was from his father. Dan had been getting a series of these. It was his only thread of hope that his father had not perished in the fire with Dan's mother, Hope Cahill. But it was not as simple as that. While Dan wanted to believe that his father was a good man and loved his children, he was far from convinced this was the case. In fact, part of Dan suspected his father of being Vesper One. If he was alive, that meant he had escaped from the fire Isabel Kabra had set. If he had escaped, that meant he had left his wife—their mother—to die in the flames. That was unforgivable.

Arthur Trent had been a nonlinear dynamics and quantum field theory professor. Dan had no real idea what that meant, but he assumed one had to be pretty smart to teach it. His father also had been a Vesper, although he had thought it was just a cool secret society and not the source of global menace. He had dropped out of West Point and been given the assignment of tracking down Hope Cahill and making her fall in love with him. But Arthur had learned some awful things about the Vespers by then. And the other thing was, he'd fallen in love with Dan's mother. For real. Renouncing the Vespers, he and Hope Cahill had spent much of their life together on the run from their enemies, namely the Vespers, who felt betrayed by Dan's father.

That was one version of the facts. But Dan could not get over the suspicion that he was being played. That his father was actually evil and working with the Vespers.

Dan looked down at the text again.

Have the serum ready, son. It may be the only thing that would allow us to be victorious.

Dan had spent a lot of time and effort collecting the strange ingredients necessary to make the formula.

He glanced at his knapsack. And in there, hidden in the depths of his other stuff, was the silver flask with the completed serum.

He surreptitiously thumbed a text back to his father.

Stop texting me. If you are alive, then you left Mom to die. If you did that, I hate you.

The response came back immediately. *I tried to save your mother. I was badly burned in the fire. I've had to go into hiding to avoid capture by the Vespers. I am working against them and with you, son. I wish I could prove it to you, but I can't. I don't blame you for being suspicious. Your mother and I taught you to be independent and look out for danger because we wanted you to be prepared But I want you to know that whatever happens, I love you and your sister. And I will do anything I can to help you. I hope one day we can all be reunited.*

As Dan read this text his heart grew heavy and his eyes misty.

He debated for a long time before answering this text.

It's ready. I will not fail. Dan.

Part of him had wanted to write, *I love you.* But he couldn't bring himself to do it. He shook his head. Life just should not be this complicated.

The reply text came back almost immediately.

Good job, Dan. I love you. And I hope to see you and your sister soon. Dad.

Dan texted back, *Okay, but if you're a Vesper, you're going down, too!!!*

Dan put his phone down and continued to stare out the window. It was very dark now. And the train slowed to twist and work its way around some hills like a snake over an obstacle course. They entered a tunnel and things became darker still.

Amy looked at him. "I say we have a powwow to discuss what we're going to do to kick the Vespers' butts."

"Sounds good to me," said Dan, avoiding the urge to glance at his knapsack, where the serum was located.

Amy picked up her phone and sent a text. A minute later there was a knock on their compartment door. She opened it, and Jake and Atticus came in and sat down.

Atticus said, "The weird happenings around the planet are getting worse. All planes are still grounded. The militaries around the world are also having to coordinate to make sure that no computer-guided warships or nuclear missiles go astray."

"Go astray!" exclaimed Amy. "A nuke going astray?"

Atticus looked at her. "Well, they're all computer-controlled systems these days. And computers are particularly sensitive to changes in magnetic fields and the overall polarity of the Earth. Accidental launches could happen."

"Well, let's hope they don't," said Jake. "We have our hands full as it is."

Amy gave him a warm smile at this comment and Jake looked back at her all goofy-eyed.

Dan saw this exchange and wrinkled his nose.

Really, their timing sucked, he thought. He said, "Okay, we're here to come up with a plan for when we get to the West Coast. All we need to do is hook up with the others, find the hostages before they're killed, locate the Doomsday device, destroy it, and capture Vesper One and all his team. Any thoughts? Anybody? Come on. How hard can it be?"

Amy said, "Your sarcasm is duly noted, Dan. But seriously, we have to have a plan." She looked at Jake.

He so desperately wanted to please her, Dan thought, that Jake might just put on a cape and try and fly off the train carrying Amy in his manly arms.

Instead, Jake said, "I'm not sure we can form a plan, Amy."

This surprised Dan. And the others.

"Why not?" she said, frowning.

"Because we don't know the conditions on the ground there. If we put this elaborate plan in place and then get there and everything is different from what we thought it would be, we'll instinctively try and execute our plan. And of course it won't work. I think the best we can do is get out there, do some recon, and then just wing it. Let the conditions we confront dictate our plan for us."

"So, we go in naked and blind?" exclaimed Dan.

"I didn't say that," replied Jake. "My point is we need to be flexible. We need to be able to zig when they think we're going to zag. We have to let our plan fit the facts, not the other way around."

"That actually makes a lot of sense," said Amy, again smiling warmly at Jake.

It also made a lot of sense to Dan, but he said nothing because he wanted to throw up at the way the two were looking at each other.

Really, what's the big deal about love, anyway?

In a sleeping car two down from them, someone else was thinking about a plan. Isabel Kabra sat in her chair and looked out the window. She believed that she had her son, Ian, back on her side. But even if he was fooling her, it didn't matter. Her plan was in place. And she had the luxury, unlike Amy and Dan, of knowing the conditions on the ground at their destination. The grounding of all flights had been very inconvenient for her, but there was nothing she could do about it.

She cursed her bad luck at having missed an opportunity to kill Amy Cahill. Really, the girl had used up more than her nine cat lives.

Isabel had no idea that two cars down Amy Cahill was thinking of the best way to beat her and the other Vespers.

But that would change.

And very soon.

CHAPTER 14

Ian Kabra was walking slowly down the dimly lit hall. He was being escorted to see his sister, Natalie. His emotions were running high right now. Seeing his mother like that, being given an order to kill. And now going to see his sister for the first time in seemingly forever. Well, it was taking its toll. He took a deep breath, trying to hold it together. And at the same time, Ian was forming a plan. A potentially brilliant plan. But also a potentially disastrous one.

Nothing like a spot of pressure, he told himself.

He had been told that Natalie had been separated from the others so that he could meet with her privately. A few seconds later a door opened and Natalie was standing there.

For all of their shallowness — such as a wild affection for Prada, Armani, and other fashion legends — and although they rarely admitted it, Ian and Natalie deeply cared for each other. Ian was now sixteen, handsome, and the son of a billionaire. He lived in London, enjoyed the finer things in life, and had gone from the dark side to the light. Part of this had to do with his crush on Amy Cahill. She had saved his life, even though she had known at the time that his mother had set the fire that had killed Amy's parents. That had struck something deep in Ian. It made him want to be a better person. He was not his mother, nor did he ever want to be.

Ian gazed at his sister. She was thirteen now. Not yet a woman, but no longer a child. She was pretty and accomplished and even more enamored of being rich than Ian was. But that would change, he thought, as she grew up.

He raced to her and held her tightly. Tears fell from both of them.

"I've missed you so much, Ian." She squeezed him so hard that he could barely breathe. But it was okay. He squeezed her back. The hug lingered, but there was a reason for this. Ian knew that they were being observed. So when Natalie started to pull away, he held her tighter.

And he started to whisper in her ear. Within thirty seconds he had told her of his dilemma. She squeezed his hand to let him know she understood. When they drew apart they looked wide-eyed at each other.

Ian smiled, trying to show her that it would be okay. When, in fact, Ian was feeling more doubt about his ability to pull this off than he had about anything else he had ever attempted. In some ways, it was far easier to be bad than good.

When you're bad, you don't care what happens to anyone other than yourself.

When you're trying to do good, you have to worry about everyone.

They were surprised when Casper prodded them out of the room without an explanation.

They walked together hand in hand down the hall, the lurking hulk of Casper right behind them. Then Casper was replaced by other guards who marched up and took charge. Casper was obviously not expecting this, but sullenly backed off when one of the guards held up his gun. The guards led Natalie and Ian down the hall to a door. One guard opened it and motioned Ian and Natalie to walk in. They did, and the door closed and locked behind them.

Ian was about to ask where the hostages were when the lights went out and a voice boomed, "What are you doing here, Ian?"

As the voice stopped ringing in his head, Ian had an epiphany. *I bet that's Vesper One. If he didn't know I'm here, then that could only mean that my mother and he are not really working together. More to the point, it means that my dear, homicidal mother is working against him and for her own purposes. As usual. She plays second fiddle to no one. And I very much doubt that she's dying of anything other than the acid that runs through her veins instead of blood.*

All the rage and anger and hatred that Ian had for his mother coalesced into a single, divine purpose.

Never fancying himself an actor, he was about to put on the performance of a lifetime.

Ian cleared his throat and said, "I'm here because my mother ordered me to come."

The voice did indeed belong to Vesper One. It once more boomed, "Your mother ordered you? I didn't think you took orders from her anymore."

"I didn't. But she can be quite persuasive, as I'm sure you know."

"And for what purpose did she order you here?"

"To kill one of the hostages. To prove my loyalty." This was easy to say for Ian, because it was the literal truth. And what he was about to say was just as truthful. He drew a deep breath and squeezed his sister's hand more tightly.

"In case you didn't realize it, my mother plans to dominate the world. And she wants my sister and me right beside her when she does it. We're her family and we're the only ones she trusts."

Ian paused and waited for a reaction from Vesper One. When there was none, he went on. "My mother warned me about others seeking to take control from her. She said there was a person out there claiming to be Vesper One. But of course my mother is Vesper One and always has been. She's the smartest of the Vespers. The most ruthless. It's her destiny to rule the world."

"Really?" said Vesper One from out of the darkness. "*She* is Vesper One?"

"Of course." Ian swallowed. It was rather

unnerving having a conversation with what seemed like a disembodied voice. "So when you go and report to her as her *subordinate* she will explain everything to you. And then she'll probably have some orders for you to carry out. Are you Vesper Two, or perhaps Three? It's quite difficult to keep the underlings straight."

Ian had said that just to dig the knife in deeper.

He waited for the voice to speak but there was just silence.

He continued, "And just so you know, Casper and Cheyenne and Sandy are working closely with my mother. So you can take orders from them as well. They have only one goal in mind: to help my mother rule the world as the true Vesper leader."

"I see," said Vesper One. "And have you picked the hostage you want to kill yet?"

The lights came back on and Ian could see all the hostages blinking and staring at him with unfriendly eyes. He had no idea where they had come from.

"Have you, Ian?" said Vesper One with amusement. "Perhaps poor little blind Ted Starling?" A spotlight hit Ted and he looked away.

"Or maybe the old fart, Fiske Cahill?"

The spotlight swung to Fiske, who just stood there defiantly. He yelled, "Just come close enough and I'll show you how hard an old fart can hit."

Vesper One continued, "Or perhaps your own dear sister?"

The spotlight beam landed on Natalie. She put up a

hand to shield her eyes from the brightness.

"I . . . I haven't quite made up my mind yet," said Ian lamely.

"Well, you'll need to do that soon. Wouldn't want to disappoint your dear chief Vesper mother."

The spotlight was turned off and the room went dark again.

Everyone waited a bit, but the voice did not come back.

Fiske Cahill called out, "Ian, you lay one hand on any of us and I'll knock you right out of your Prada."

"For your information, I'm wearing Ralph Lauren," snapped Ian. He drew closer, groping in the darkness. He whispered, "And it was just an act. I'm on your side."

"Right!" barked Nellie. "We all heard what you said about killing one of us."

"I had to tell my mother that or she never would have allowed me in here. I wanted to get Vesper One and my mother doubting each other instead of focusing on us."

Ted whispered, "That's actually a smart strategy."

They all drew closer in the dark until they were standing next to one another.

"Is everyone okay?" asked Ian.

"Everyone except Alistair. He's dead," said Fiske.

"I know," replied Ian quietly. "It's simply shocking. What did he die of?"

"Being brutalized by a bunch of cowards," snapped Fiske.

DAY OF DOOM

"Is Amy okay?" asked Nellie anxiously.

"I know that she barely survived an attack from my mother."

"What are you doing here?" barked Fiske.

"Evan and I flew out here to join up with Phoenix. He got a call through to Attleboro when we were there."

"Phoenix made it out? He's okay?" exclaimed Reagan. "We thought he died in the fall."

"He was perfectly all right until we all were captured by the Wyomings and Sandy. Hamilton and Jonah are prisoners, too," said Ian miserably. "They're locked in a room close to this one."

"Hamilton?" said Reagan. "Is he all right?"

"For now. Like all of us. But I can't believe that will last. Something's going on out there. Planes are having a hard time flying. I think it might be tied to the Vespers' plan somehow."

"Where are Amy and Dan?" whispered Nellie.

"On their way. At least I think they are. The only question is, will they be in time?"

Vesper One had returned to his chambers to mull over what Ian had told him. Some of it was surprising. Some of it he had suspected. He finally made a decision. Well, he actually made two decisions.

He had an ace in the hole with Isabel. She was a true Vesper, meaning the only person she looked out for was herself.

The other decision was easy enough to implement. It was time to move the hostages, including the additional five they had just collected.

He didn't want them to miss out on the finale. They all had to be there.

And in his heart, black as it was, he knew that Amy and Dan would be in attendance as well.

Atticus had been right.

That was just the way it had to end.

CHAPTER 15

The Capitol Limited train pulled into Chicago's Union Station at a little after eleven o'clock the following morning. Dan yawned and looked out the window. He had slept better than he thought he would in the top bunk. A few times the train rocked so hard that he had to brace himself against the wall, but other than that the gentle swaying had let him forget the danger they were heading toward and allowed him to get some much-needed rest.

He looked down from his high perch and saw his sister sitting in the chair. She'd washed her face in the tiny collapsible sink and changed her clothes in the little bathroom in the compartment that also housed a shower. Their bags were packed and ready to go. Dan saw that she had laid out some clothes for him to wear.

She looked up and saw him staring at her. "They apparently have to back into the station," she said. "So it'll take a little longer. Time for you to wash up and change your clothes."

"What about food?"

"We can get some breakfast in the station."

While the train was doing its last bit of maneuvering, Dan washed up and changed into fresh clothes. He had kept his knapsack containing the flask with the serum in it next to him while he slept. He put this over his shoulder and followed Amy down the narrow corridor and out of the car, after the conductor announced it was time to detrain.

As soon as they were on the station platform, Jake and Atticus joined them. Jake looked sleepy while Atticus seemed energized.

"Okay," Amy began. "We have quite a while before the train leaves for Seattle. We'll get some breakfast, try to contact the others, and get up to speed with any new global developments. I'm assuming the Internet connection inside the station will be better than it was on the train."

"Let's hope so," exclaimed Dan. "I'm going through information withdrawal."

Jake yawned.

Amy looked at him and smiled. "Not enough sleep?"

"Not enough something," he replied. "I'll feel better after I eat."

Dan found a food court inside the station. He was coming back to get the others when he saw it.

Or rather, *her.*

Oh, no, thought Dan.

He ran ahead, grabbed Amy's arm, and pulled her

down a side hall. He motioned for Jake and Atticus to follow.

"What is it?" Amy asked in an annoyed tone.

Dan poked his head around the corner and said, "Look."

They all peered around the corner. Atticus gulped. Jake did not look sleepy anymore. Dan simply looked furious. And Amy thought once more of how close she had come to dying.

Isabel Kabra and her guards were marching down the main hall of the station.

Dan whispered, "Here she is, trying to destroy the world, and she's marching around like she owns the place. While *we* have to hide from *her*."

Amy nodded. "It does seem pretty unfair. But we have to hide from her because she'll definitely try to kill us if she gets the chance."

"Criminals have it so easy," complained Dan. "No moral dilemmas, no soul-searching. Just kill, kill, kill."

"Do you really want to be a criminal?" asked Amy, staring hard at him.

"I didn't say that," replied Dan indignantly. "My point is it's harder to be the good guys."

"And *better* to be the good guys," added Atticus.

"Well, of course you'd think that," said Dan. "You're a Guardian. You come from centuries of good guys. It's part of your DNA."

Jake said, "She's heading into the first-class lounge. Which means we can't go in there."

"Great," said Dan. "Criminals get first-class lounges and we get zip. Fast food and hard chairs."

"Look out," said Jake. "One of her goons is coming this way."

"Scatter," said Amy.

They all turned and moved away in different directions. They let the man pass and then regrouped at a spot far removed from the first-class lounge.

There were big windows in the train station near the food court. As they hastily ate breakfast, Dan continuously glanced out the windows.

"That is like no sky I've ever seen," said Dan.

The others glanced out of the windows. The clouds were formed into shapes that were most definitely not ordinary. The color of the sky was a pale yellow, but there were undertones of darker colors all around that one also did not associate with the sky.

"There's nothing we can do about that right now," said Amy. "But we have to put together a plan for Isabel."

"Okay," said Dan. "I have one."

"What is it?" asked his sister.

"We wait until the train is moving really fast on its way to Seattle and then we open the door and throw Isabel off."

Jake looked at Amy. "That's actually not a bad plan."

"I could go for it, too," added Atticus.

"It's a terrible plan," said Amy.

"What?" exclaimed Dan.

"Isabel being here is actually great for us."

Dan said, "Amy, do you need to have your brain checked? The last time you ran into that witch, she nearly killed you."

"I know that. But now we have the upper hand."

"Why?" asked Jake.

"Because she doesn't know we're here. Which means we can use Isabel to lead us to the hostages."

"How?" asked all three of the guys in unison.

"Why do you think Isabel is on this train?" she said in a tone of *I can't believe you all are that dense.*

Amy continued when none of them seemed prepared to answer.

"She's on the train heading to Seattle. To hook up with the Vespers. She had to take the train just like we did, because the planes aren't flying. If we follow her, she will lead us right to the hostages. We won't have to waste time tracking them down. It's perfect."

The three guys looked at one another. Jake said, "Yeah, I guess you're right."

Atticus concurred, too.

Dan was the last to nod in agreement, but his thoughts were already elsewhere. He touched his knapsack, where the flask of serum was hidden.

He would be prepared, he told himself. Whatever happened, the Vespers were not going to win.

And the world was not going to end.

Not on my watch, Dan told himself. *Not on my watch.*

CHAPTER 16

"Are you scared?"

Amy looked over at Jake as she asked the question.

They were hiding out in the cavernous train station. Atticus and Dan were in another part of the building, keeping out of sight of Isabel and her cohorts. They kept in contact via texts. Amy had thought it smarter to split up. That way all of them could not be captured together.

She and Jake were in an old supply closet that had a broken door lock. They figured no one would be coming in to get supplies because the room was empty. They felt safe, at least reasonably so.

Jake sat on the floor while Amy perched against a wooden shelf nailed to one wall.

He said, "I guess I'd be a moron if I wasn't scared."

She nodded. "And we both know you're not a moron." She smiled to show she was just kidding.

He grinned back. "It's nice to know you can keep things light when surrounded by danger and the potential for the destruction of the world."

"Hey, girls like to laugh," she said.

"I hope I get lots of chances in the future to make you laugh, Amy."

He rose and leaned back against the wall opposite her.

"You've made me laugh in the past," she replied, looking uncomfortable.

"Like I said, I'm talking about the *future*."

She blushed and looked down. "Jake, you know that I really like you."

"But I hear a *but* coming."

She looked up. "But." She smiled miserably. "But it's not that simple."

"Meaning there's Evan?"

"Evan's a great guy, too."

"I know he is. And I know it's not an easy decision, Amy. But at some point you have to make one."

"Now, in the middle of all this? That's hardly fair."

He moved a little closer. "There's nothing fair about love, Ames. It doesn't run on a neat schedule. You can't turn it on and off." He paused and added, "At least *I* can't."

"Jake—" she began before he put up a hand to forestall her comment.

"I've been thinking a lot about this, Amy. And saying what's in my heart now makes a lot of sense actually, precisely because we're in the situation we're in."

"You mean because we might not make it out alive?"

He nodded and drew another inch closer. "So here goes. I could make it all ooey-gooey and sappy, but that's not how I feel, Amy. What's in my heart is clean and simple and straightforward." He drew himself up to his full height, towering over her even as she shrank back a bit.

"I love you, Amy Cahill. I've known it for a long time. Maybe from the moment I saw you. And my feelings have only gotten stronger."

Amy's eyes began to tear up. "Oh, Jake."

"You don't have to answer me back. But now I've said it. So whatever happens, you'll know."

She flung herself into his arms and held him tight.

"Jake, I love you, too. I think I've known it for a long time as well."

They looked at each other, their faces, their lips barely inches apart.

And then they kissed.

When they drew apart he said, "You've just made my whole life."

"I was sort of thinking the same thing."

Jake grinned and said, "Pretty weird place and time to discuss the future. An empty supply closet in the middle of a train station, while we're waiting for the world to maybe end. So for an encore let's go find a dumpster and really start getting serious about our relationship."

Amy laughed. "See, you just made me do it. Laugh."

He grinned and held her tighter. "You think we'll make it through this?"

"If we stick together, I think we have a good shot."

"I'll stick with you, Ames. Whatever happens I'll have your back. You know that, right?"

"Yeah, I do. And I've got yours."

It was stuffy in there. Amy could feel herself growing warm. And this made her think of something not quite so pleasant.

"Jake, if anything happens to me—"

He gripped her tighter and said, "Amy, don't."

"We have to be realistic about this, okay? So if anything happens to me and I don't make it out of this alive, can I count on you to take care of Dan?"

Jake looked down, his eyes moistening. Amy noticed this and she felt her eyes tear up, too.

"I will take care of Dan. You have no worries there."

"Thanks."

"Will you do the same for Atticus?"

"Of course," she said in a hushed voice.

"But I want you to know that I will die for you, Amy. I will die so that no harm comes to you."

She blushed. "I know," she said in barely a whisper.

"Can we stop being so depressed now?" he asked.

She hugged him back. "Yeah. Sounds good."

Jake was starting to kiss her again when Amy's phone buzzed.

"I better get that," she said.

"Can't it wait?"

She pulled the phone from her pocket and glanced at the screen.

"It's Dan."

Jake was still holding her. "Just one more minute." His lips dipped to hers.

She jerked back.

"Hey, my kiss wouldn't be that bad," complained Jake.

"It's not that. Something's going on in the center of the station. Dan said to come now!"

She raced out of the storage closet.

Jake stared at Amy wearily, then hustled after her.

Sometimes a guy just can't win.

A voice was booming over the station PA system.

Jake had caught up to Amy before she reached the center of the station.

"Amy, what's going on?" he asked. "Who's that talking?"

"Over here," said a voice.

They both turned and saw Dan motioning to them from a corner of the long hall. "This way," he said urgently.

They ran over to him. Atticus was also there.

"This way, quick," said Dan.

"What's that loud voice?" asked Jake as they ran along.

"It's coming from a press conference," said Atticus.

"Loudspeaker system piped throughout the station."

"It's being held in the middle of the station," added Dan.

"A press conference? Who's holding it?" asked Amy.

"You're never going to believe it," exclaimed Atticus.

"These days I'll believe anything," she countered.

"It's Isabel Kabra," replied Dan. "She's holding a press conference on AWW. This should really be good."

As they ran toward the center of the station, the voice grew louder and louder.

CHAPTER 17

He stood in front of a large, ornate mirror that hung on one wall and studied himself. He wasn't tall, at least in stature. About five-six. His hair was brown and wavy. His build was slight. But he was wiry, with more strength inside him than showed from his frame. His features were sharp, pugnacious— some would say ratlike. But people who thought he resembled a rodent were just jealous. And besides, what he looked like was just wallpaper.

What counted was what was on the inside. He came from a long line of great men.

"My name is Damien Vesper," he said to the reflection, and as the words came out of his mouth he smiled and his chest swelled with pride.

"And my father was Damien Vesper."

He smiled again.

"And we are both directly related to the first Damien Vesper, who gallantly battled and defeated Gideon Cahill all those centuries ago."

His smile now spanned his face as he recalled his

family's domination of the Cahills.

At least, that's how the Vespers saw it. And that was the crux of it. Vespers were winners. They always had been and they always would be. Which meant the Cahills, despite their wealth and status, would always be losers.

He had risen to be Vesper One at the tender age of twenty-three, not by birthright, although that should count for something, but rather by ability. He was, simply, the most ruthless of all the Vespers, willing to do anything, kill anyone, to accomplish his goals.

He lifted his sleeve, revealing the large burn on his arm. It was ugly, still painful, but he wore it as a badge of honor. He could take the pain. He could bear the wounds, because he came from greatness.

But as spectacular as his bloodline was, he planned to surpass them all to become the greatest Vesper of all.

He turned away from the mirror and continued to turn things over in his head.

Damien Vesper was superb at brooding. He found it useful to think things through. Also, he liked to be alone. He did not care for people, really. Which was one reason he had no qualms about killing lots of them. For him, most people didn't deserve to live. They were useless, pathetic losers taking up precious space on a chunk of rock moving in slow circles in the solar system around a boiling mass of energy called the sun. For Damien Vesper, it was time to do some serious pruning of the human race. And he now had the means to do so.

He had constructed this little chamber as a personal retreat. It actually was built to mirror the private chamber of King Louis XVI. The little king married to the beautiful Marie Antoinette was a favorite model for Damien. He liked the king's arrogance, his disregard for others. He liked his unquenchable thirst for power and the fact that he did not care in the least who was hurt by it. This was a world where one had to look out for oneself. And those who were clearly superior to others must have no reservations about exerting that superiority.

However, he did not want to share the king's fate. Being beheaded by guillotine by French revolutionaries was not how he wanted to leave the world. He was not afraid of death. He simply wanted to go out on his own terms.

He rose and looked out the window. What was staring back at him was stark and foreboding. It had truly begun. Damien had imposed his will on the very planet. The strange-looking sky, the unpredictable winds, magnetic fields gone haywire: Mother Nature herself was under his power.

But now there were decisions to be made. Disloyalty could not be tolerated. Ian Kabra had given Damien, stupidly enough, valuable information about his mother. Damien had always harbored doubts about Vesper Two. It was a known fact that if anyone rivaled him for sheer, audacious, unbridled ambition, it was Isabel Kabra. Yet the foolish woman should have worked harder to maintain the secrecy of her ambitions. She was acting as though Vesper One were incompetent.

She thinks she can take advantage of me because I'm young and she believes me unfit to lead the Vespers. She will find out how wrong she is. I am young. But I am more than qualified to lead. Indeed, it is my destiny. And she will not rob me of it.

He would need to purge the traitors from his ranks. It actually wouldn't be that difficult. Damien knew what lurked inside other Vespers. He knew how they thought, how they reacted to situations. What they feared. He knew all this because he was a Vesper like no other.

Yes, he would take care of those who sought to destroy him. But then his thoughts turned to Amy and Dan, his sworn enemies. The Cahills were weak. In the end, they would be no match for him. But other Vespers in the past had fallen to overconfidence. He would not give them a chance to strike him a mortal blow. Indeed, thanks to them he had all that he needed to complete the Doomsday device. The world was already feeling the effects of the machine, though Damien had not fully engaged it. The ancient Archimedes invention was a true marvel. Its destructive power was nearly unimaginable.

I look forward to seeing what it can really do.

Damien walked to the door. He had something to do. Something very important. Then again, everything he did was important.

Soon the world would know very well what Damien Vesper was capable of. They soon also would know of his greatness.

From a safe distance, Amy and the others were watching in disbelief as Isabel did her thing.

"The sheer gall of that woman never ceases to amaze me," said a goggle-eyed Amy, as she watched Isabel perform for the crowd gathered around her.

Isabel's amplified voice boomed out while a large sign painted with the letters *AWW* hung behind her on the makeshift stage.

"Dark days are coming, my friends," said Isabel, who stood in the center of the stage with a microphone in hand. "Things will be happening that you will not understand. I don't understand them, either. One look at the skies will confirm that an apocalypse is upon us. There will be no guarantees exactly what the future will bring. But one thing I can guarantee you, my friends, is that I, Isabel Kabra, and my organization, AWW, or Aid Works Wonders, will be there for you."

Some people in the crowd started to clap and cheer.

"Hey," said Dan. "Those are Isabel's guys."

"They're there to get the crowd fired up," said Amy. "It's an old trick."

"And it's working," added Atticus.

The rest of the crowd indeed began cheering Isabel as she continued telling them all the good she would do for them.

After she finished speaking, a flock of reporters rushed the stage and started asking Isabel questions. She faced them with a big smile and an attractive tilt to her head.

One reporter asked, "What danger do you foresee, Ms. Kabra?"

She turned to him and looked directly at a large video camera that another man was holding. "If one could foresee danger, it would largely cease to be a danger," said Isabel smoothly. "What we will need to be is vigilant, diligent, and persistent."

"Anything else?" asked another journalist.

"Of course. The most important element of all. Leadership. I will be happy to serve. I want all of you to look to me when the time comes. Remember who warned you. Remember who guaranteed that she would be there for you. Even the loss of *one* life cannot be tolerated. It's far too precious."

"I'm going to vomit, I swear I am," said Dan from his hiding place.

"I'm right there with you," said Amy. "'Far too

precious'? Just yesterday she was trying pretty hard to end one life. Mine!"

Atticus pointed to a large window. "Look!"

They all turned to gaze out.

"What?" asked Dan.

"I saw a bolt of lightning," said Atticus.

"So?" said Dan dismissively. "It does happen, you know. It's called a *storm*!"

At that moment another bolt of lightning appeared in the sky. Only it was shooting upward, not down to the earth.

The others stared, openmouthed, while Atticus gazed pointedly at Dan.

"Oh," said Dan sheepishly. "That's, uh, that's not good."

"Ya think?" exclaimed Atticus.

An announcement was broadcast over the station PA system.

"They're calling our train," said Amy. "Let's go. But make sure Isabel doesn't spot us."

They took great pains to make sure they got on the train without Isabel or her people seeing them. However, they were so focused on Isabel that they failed to see someone else watching *them*. As Amy and Dan got into one car and Jake and Atticus into another, this person climbed aboard a car that was in between them.

Sinead Starling pulled her hat down low and took her seat for the long ride ahead.

CHAPTER 18

"Stupid train," exclaimed Jake.

He and Atticus were sitting in Amy and Dan's compartment. Jake was working on his laptop but his Internet connection kept failing.

"How can something like this happen in the twenty-first century?" he wanted to know.

Amy was looking out the window at the passing scenery. With all the worries she had, Amy seemed at peace. It might have been the beautiful landscape she was watching as the train made its way to the West Coast. Or it might have been that she was resigned to whatever fate would befall her. Perhaps she didn't really even know for sure.

She said, "I sort of like the train. At least you can see things you can't at thirty-five thousand feet."

"Yeah, but apparently you can't get a solid Internet connection," complained Jake. He looked at his screen. "Okay, I'm back on. Excuse me while I do some digital sleuthing."

Dan, who was watching Amy watch Jake with a

lovey-dovey expression, rolled his eyes, sighed, and sat back in his seat. Dan could tell this was going to be a very, very long ride. He snatched a glance at Atticus. He really liked Atticus, but the last official Guardian on earth could become very stoic on occasion. This appeared to be one of those occasions as he silently looked out the window.

"Is that snow?" exclaimed Amy.

They all looked outside, all except Jake, who was still glued to his laptop screen.

Dan said, "How can it be snowing? It was seventy-five degrees in Chicago. And we're not that far from there." He quickly checked his phone's weather app.

"It's thirty degrees out there! How can the temperature drop forty-five degrees just like that?"

Then Dan blinked, and the snow seemed to simply vanish. "Okay, I am big-time freaking out now." As he continued to watch, a thunderstorm started up. But, like back in Chicago, the lightning was shooting upward. Dan gripped his seat and paled. Isabel Kabra, curse her, had been right that the apocalypse was coming. In fact, it was apparently already here. As they continued to stare out the window, all those meteorological anomalies disappeared and the sky cleared.

Atticus pointed to a distant hill. "Look!"

As they watched, the mound of dirt trembled and then came crashing down, taking some houses, and no doubt people, with it.

The train roared on.

"Was that an earthquake?" asked Amy. "I didn't feel anything."

"The whole world has gone crazy," said Dan.

"No," announced Jake.

They all gaped at him.

He was finally looking up from his laptop.

"The world has not gone crazy. In fact, it's starting to make a lot of sense."

Dan peeked over at Amy, who was looking all gooey-eyed again at Jake. Dan groaned. He'd had enough.

Dan snapped, "Okay, Mr. Genius, why don't you enlighten us morons as to exactly what all makes sense?"

So focused was Jake on the data on his computer that he didn't appear to have gotten Dan's sarcasm at all. This seemed, to Dan, to be a genetic problem with the Rosenblooms.

Jake said amiably, "Glad to."

He spun his laptop around so they could all see the screen.

"I've been researching both the historical accounts of Archimedes' inventions, and the elements that we were forced to gather by Vesper One. I did a spreadsheet analysis that attempted to make sense of both the elements' potential use and the plans that Archimedes had for his devices. I was, in effect, searching for a pattern."

"Well, can you search faster?" complained Dan. "Because the world is coming to an end, bud, in case you haven't noticed."

"Dan," said Amy in an admonishing tone. "What Jake has done looks brilliant." She flashed Jake a huge smile. Poor Jake looked on the verge of melting under its wattage.

"Go on, Jake," said Amy encouragingly.

"Oh, give me a freaking break," muttered Dan under his breath.

Jake continued. "What I found was that the Doomsday device, constructed with the aid of all the elements we gathered, has the potential not merely to disrupt the Earth's magnetic field, but also to *reverse* the polarity of the magnetic poles of the Earth entirely."

"And that's bad?" said Dan.

"It could be catastrophic," answered Jake. "Reversing the polarity of the magnetic poles could result in unprecedented loss. It's no wonder that all the planes were grounded. In fact, very soon the entire Internet might crash."

"Well, we knew that Vesper One had already activated the Doomsday device," said Atticus.

"Yeah," added Dan. "All the crazy weather, the planes, stuff like that? He had to have pulled the trigger. It's the only explanation."

"I still think that Vesper One is only doing a trial run," Jake said. "He deliberately hasn't activated the device to its full power yet. If he had, I think we'd see a lot worse than we have so far."

"How can you be sure of that?" asked Amy.

"Fully reversing the magnetic poles of the Earth

would cause catastrophic damage the likes of which we have never seen before, Amy. Tsunamis striking land on the East Coast. Dozens of hurricanes forming simultaneously in the Pacific. Earthquakes where earthquakes have never happened before. Increased volcanic activity. It could potentially even take the Earth out of its proper orbit. It could turn the world literally upside down."

"And destroy it?" she said in a hushed tone.

"Absolutely. It could even interrupt the actual gravitational forces of the Earth. And if that happens, there would be no guarantee that anything would be left to hold us onto the planet."

The others instinctively gripped their armrests as though to keep themselves firmly on Earth.

"Well," said Dan. "I guess that's sort of the point of a Doomsday device. You know, *doomsday*!" He glanced surreptitiously at his knapsack, where the flask containing the serum was hidden.

Amy said, "But as evil as he is, why would Vesper One want to destroy the world? He lives on it, too."

Atticus piped up. "It must be that he thinks if he demonstrates that he has the ability to cause such devastation he can blackmail the rest of the world into doing his bidding."

Dan said, "Exactly. The guy is going to use this threat to make himself supreme ruler of everything. And that would suck big-time, because the guy is obviously a jerk."

Amy said, "And that explains what Isabel was doing back there. Her organization will reap enormous benefits if she's ahead of the curve on this. She'll pretend to clean up the mess she helped cause. The people will love her when they should be arresting her."

"That witch," snapped Dan.

Amy stared at the laptop screen. "And from what we know about subduction zones, the Cascade Mountains are the perfect place to set off the device and show the world the power Vesper One has." She paused. "And that also explains the location of the hostages."

"What do you mean?" asked Jake.

She looked at him. "They're going to bury the hostages under what's left of the Cascade Mountains when they turn on the device full blast."

They all stared at one another.

Amy said, "Now the question is, how do we stop it?"

As the train rattled on, no one seemed to have an answer.

CHAPTER 19

It was very late at night. The train was rolling on toward Colorado.

Inside the compartment where Jake and Atticus were staying, Jake slept soundly.

Atticus was having a much tougher time of it. He tossed and turned, tried deep breathing, counted backward, but nothing worked. He finally sat up in his top bunk, drew aside the curtain, and looked out the window. He had no idea where they were. All he could see was darkness and the silhouettes of landscapes zooming by. And then Atticus started thinking about his mother.

Astrid Rosenbloom had been full of health and vitality until she had started going rapidly downhill. The doctors could never figure out exactly what was wrong with her. But now it seemed to Atticus — based on what he had observed — that the doctors were always being reactive to his mother's conditions. They had treated the effects of her illnesses. But they had not focused all that much on the cause. They had run many tests, to be sure, but had they run enough of them? And had they run the right ones?

It now seemed so simple that Atticus couldn't believe he hadn't thought of it before.

And I'm supposed to have such a big brain.

When someone became ill and continued to sink despite everything the doctors could do, and no cause was ever found, there often was a good explanation for that.

And a criminal one.

His mother had started feeling bad not that long after she had gained a new research assistant, Dave Speminer. And the whole time that assistant was with her, Astrid Rosenbloom had become sicker and sicker. And that assistant would have been in an ideal place to administer a poison even after she was being cared for by the doctors, because he came to visit her often.

Am I paranoid?

Dave Speminer? Dave Speminer?

There was something about that name that was bugging him. And then he got an idea. Of course, ideas came to Atticus all the time. But he had a feeling about this one.

Atticus closed the curtain, picked up his phone, and began hitting buttons.

His phone had a Scrabble app. He brought it up and typed in the name *Dave Speminer*. There was something about that name that seemed familiar, if one looked at it in a different way.

A few seconds later Atticus was proved right. *Dave Speminer* was an anagram. The Scrabble app took the name *Dave Speminer* and turned it into another name.

Damien Vesper.

Dave Speminer was Damien Vesper. Dave Speminer had murdered Atticus's mother.

And then Atticus, his huge brain firing on all cylinders, made another leap of logic.

While not all anagrams of *Damien Vesper*, Atticus was sure that Damien Vesper, Riley McGrath, and Dave Speminer were one and the same. It just made sense based on all the facts.

And one of those "facts" hit Atticus like an artillery round. His eyes filled with tears. The man his mother had trusted had killed her. And that man had been the dreaded head of the Vesper clan. He wiped his eyes and cleared the tears away. His mouth set in a firm line. Now was not the time for grieving or sadness or despair. Now was the time for action, for justice. And yes, for revenge. He climbed down off his bunk and woke Jake.

His big brother looked very annoyed at having his sleep interrupted.

Atticus had heard Jake in his sleep say the name *Amy* more than once. He had to hide a smile as Jake looked at him.

But when Atticus showed Jake his cell phone and the results of the Scrabble app, Jake sat up so fast he hit his head on the underside of the top bunk.

Rubbing his head and looking cross, he said, "I'll get dressed and get Amy and Dan. You stay here."

As Jake was getting dressed, Atticus sat in the chair by the window and gazed out. Atticus finally looked over at his brother.

"We have to get him, Jake," said Atticus.

"I know," said Jake as he buttoned up his shirt.

"He killed Mom."

"I know, Atticus, I know."

"We'll get him, right? Make him pay?"

Jake laced up his shoes and then put a hand on his little brother's arm. "We'll get him, Att. I promise you that."

Jake knocked lightly on the door of Amy and Dan's compartment. Amy opened the door, dressed in sweats. Her hair was tousled, her eyes puffy with sleep, and yet to Jake she looked beautiful.

"Is everything okay?" she asked nervously. "Where's Atticus?"

"Everything's okay," said Jake softly. "But Att has figured out something, and you all need to hear it. Can you get dressed and come on?"

"Give us a couple of minutes."

Jake waited outside the door, ever mindful that Isabel Kabra and her men were on this train as well. However, no one passed by except a female conductor who looked vaguely familiar to Jake, but he figured it was because he had seen her pass by earlier in the day.

He didn't look again at the woman.

Sinead Starling never glanced back, either. The wily Ekat with nerves the size of Alaska kept walking until she reached another train car and passed through into it.

A few minutes later, Amy and Dan, fully dressed, were following Jake down the hall to his compartment.

Dan yawned and said, "This better be good, Jake. I was dreaming about feeding Isabel and Vesper One to the sharks. And feeling sorry. For the *sharks*."

They reached the other compartment and Jake slid the door closed behind them. Atticus was sitting on the lower bunk. Jake sat beside him, and Dan and Amy sat in chairs opposite.

"So what's up, Atticus?" asked Amy.

He quickly explained about the Scrabble app and showed them the results on the screen.

Atticus said, "It can't be a coincidence about the names being an anagram. The odds are billions to one."

Amy nodded. "You're right. So Dave Speminer, your mother's assistant, is Vesper One."

Dan eyed Atticus sadly. "And that means he killed your mom?"

Atticus slowly nodded as he gazed back at Dan.

They had always had a special bond, both having lost their mothers. But now that bond had deepened.

They both had lost their mothers violently and prematurely to the Vespers.

Jake said, "So this sort of confirms, doesn't it, that Isabel isn't Vesper One?"

"It does," said Amy.

Atticus added, "And Dave Speminer is young, much younger than Isabel."

"Ooohhh, Isabel must really hate that," said Dan. "Taking orders from basically a kid."

"When I was goading her in that alley in DC, I could see how badly she wanted to be the leader in all this," said Amy. "Her blind ambition might give us an opportunity."

"What do you mean, Am?" asked Jake.

"That she'll do anything to become Vesper One."

"Including knocking off Vesper One?" said Dan.

She gazed at him. "You know as well as I do that Isabel will kill anyone to get what she wants."

"Yes, she will," agreed Dan.

"Well," said Atticus, "she's on the train right now."

"Yeah, which makes me very nervous," said Jake. "If she spots us, we are dead."

Atticus continued, "What I was thinking was that we might turn her being here into an advantage."

"How?" asked Dan.

"If we can search her compartment, there might be something in there that could help us."

"But we don't know which one is her compartment," said Amy.

Dan held up his phone. "Already hacked into Amtrak's reservation system. She's in Train Car A, Compartment Three."

"But, search her compartment?" exclaimed Jake. "We'll get caught for sure."

"Not if we can create a diversion," said Atticus.

Amy said, "Atticus, do you really think the risk is worth it?"

Atticus took a moment before answering. "I've given this a lot of thought, Amy. I am the last Guardian and it's my job to stop the Vespers. But now it's *personal*. He murdered my mom. So nothing will stop me from beating the Vespers. And I'm tired of just reacting to whatever the Vespers do."

Jake added, "Yeah, they have had us running around, doing all of their dirty work for them."

"Amen to that, brother," said Dan.

They all looked at him curiously.

He said sheepishly, "I've been watching movies from the eighties on my laptop. They said that line a lot way back then. I'm not really sure why."

"But we still need a diversion," noted Jake.

Atticus smiled. "I have a plan for that. A really cool one."

"Amen to that, bro," said Dan.

Atticus held up a fist. "Word."

They all looked at one another and then started roaring with laughter. Even under the dire circumstances it just seemed like the right thing to do.

CHAPTER 20

Isabel Kabra sat alone in her private compartment. She was staring into the mirror over the tiny sink that made up part of her lavatory.

She never had ridden on an American train before. First class or private planes had always been part of her world. And luxurious train travel in Europe. As the pampered wife of a billionaire, she had always assumed that the world would literally be at her feet. She was appalled at having to travel this way, and with ordinary people so close around her. Why, a man in a uniform had come in and said it was time to go to the dining car to eat.

To eat with ordinary people!

She would have shot him for his insolence, if she could have figured out a way to dispose of the body.

And then there was the tiniest of bathrooms in the compartment. It doubled as both a toilet and a shower! She was sure to the peons of the world— meaning pretty much everyone except herself—it was just fine. But to her it was unthinkable. She shuddered at even the thought of wedging her perfect self into that minuscule space both to pee and to bathe.

But the train it had to be. Her private jet had attempted to take off from Washington DC after that fiasco involving Amy Cahill in that alley. But after repeated attempts her pilots had reported that they could not safely get into the air.

She couldn't believe that the Cahills had actually called in the police in DC. That was not playing fair at all. The battle was between the Vespers and the Cahills. It was a family matter. It should be kept in the family. She would make Amy's and Dan's deaths a million times more painful to make up for that insult.

She looked over some of her AWW materials. She smiled. What a brilliant subterfuge, and the idiots ate it up like chocolate. But once she dethroned Vesper One, AWW would be an important element of her overall plan. Vesper One, the snot, could never be this subtle. Subtle? Ha! He was about as subtle as a charging rhinoceros.

But that would work to her advantage.

She looked at her watch. Two in the morning. She should get some sleep. She had to keep up her beauty rest, even in the midst of her quest for total and complete world domination.

After all, a girl had to look her best if she was planning on ruling the world.

And Isabel had always been beautiful. All the men thought so. Even ones who were her sworn enemies.

And all the women were jealous of her looks, she was well aware of that. But then again, people were always intimidated by perfection.

She studied her face in the mirror once more. She then looked closer.

Was that a wrinkle?

The lights in her compartment went out. She jerked up so suddenly, she hit her head on the little overhead light.

Trembling with rage, she screamed into her cell phone, "Here. Now!"

The door to her compartment flew open and two of her men stood there.

"Yes, Mrs. Kabra?" said one of them nervously. "Is there a problem?"

"A problem?" she began sweetly. "Why, just a teensy-weensy one." Then she roared, "The lights went out, you idiot. Find out why! And I hit my head. I'm going to sue whoever owns this crummy train."

"I think the Americans own it," said the other guard meekly.

"Great," grumbled Isabel. "They don't have any money to pay damages."

The PA system crackled and a voice came on.

"All passengers, there has been an electrical system interruption on the train. Please make your way to the dining car, where flashlights and emergency instructions will be given out. All passengers, please make your way to the dining car at once. Thank you."

"I'm not going to any dining car," snapped Isabel.

The PA system crackled again. "Any passenger attempting to stay in his seat or compartment will be escorted off the train at the next stop. No exceptions."

Isabel fumed for a few moments and then snatched her bag. "I will kill whoever caused the electrical interruption." She pointed to one of her men. "Find out who the person is and write the name down for me. And be sure to get the correct spelling."

"Yes, Mrs. Kabra."

She stomped down the hall.

"Uh, Mrs. Kabra?" said one of her guards.

She turned and yelled, "What!"

"The dining car is the other way," the man said timidly.

Isabel Kabra gave a prolonged sigh, marched over to him, slugged him in the face with her bag, and stomped toward the dining car. She called back over her shoulder, "And don't forget that name! Or I'll kill you, too."

Atticus and Jake were standing in a control room on the train, located in a vestibule between two cars. Jake had picked the lock to get inside, and Atticus had powered down the train's electrical system, except for low-level emergency lighting. He had then turned on the train's PA system to make the announcement in the deepest voice he could muster. Finally, he had disabled the PA system so that no more announcements could be made, at least for a while.

"So cool, Att," said Jake admiringly.

"Just a simple case of reverse engineering," replied Atticus modestly. "But now comes the hard part."

"Right. Come on. We need to be nearby while Amy and Dan search Isabel's compartment, just in case anything goes wrong. Which it probably will."

They waited until the other passengers had passed by them on the way to the dining car before racing down the hall toward Isabel's compartment.

Dan and Amy were right outside Isabel's compartment. They looked at each other. Dan peeked inside the window.

"Coast is clear."

Amy said, "We probably have only a few minutes before Isabel realizes this was all a scam."

Dan answered by yanking open the door. "So let's get it done."

They moved inside and Dan shut the door behind them. They used penlights to look around the darkened room. Dan dug through Isabel's suitcase and toiletry bag.

"Yuck," he said.

"What is it?" whispered Amy.

He held up a long plastic folding case. "Have you ever seen this much makeup in your life? And she has ten pairs of eyebrow tweezers."

"Haven't you ever seen her brows? Without those tweezers it would be a big furry caterpillar right across her forehead."

Dan put the case back and kept searching.

"Dan, look at this."

He hurried over to her. Amy had been searching a bag that had been stowed in a storage cabinet next to the tiny bathroom.

She held up photos and shone her light on them.

"Those are pictures of the Lewis and Clark compass," exclaimed Dan.

"Exactly."

The pictures were of both the front and rear of the compass, just like they had taken at the museum, too.

"It was just like the lady at the museum said," commented Amy.

Dan shot his hand down into the bag and pulled out a phone.

"Why would she have her phone in a bag in storage?" said Dan.

"Maybe it's a backup phone," answered Amy. "Anything on it?"

Dan hit some buttons and his face turned pale. "Yeah," he said quietly.

"What?"

He held up the phone. On it were several texts. Texts sent to Dan. And they were all signed *AJT.*

Amy looked at Dan. He said, "AJT. Arthur Josiah Trent. The texts I thought I was receiving from Dad were actually from that witch." He looked up miserably at Amy. "I know you always thought they were fake."

"It doesn't make it any easier for you, Dan. I wanted Mom and Dad alive, too. And I didn't want Dad to be a Vesper. And I don't believe he was."

Dan put the phone back in the bag. "Well, I guess this proves that Dad wasn't a bad guy. He wasn't with the Vespers. He never left Mom in that house. They died together."

Amy was about to say something when her phone buzzed.

It was a frantic text from Jake. Isabel was on her way back. They had to get out of the compartment right now.

They both turned toward the door just as the train hit a big bump. The door partially slid open and then banged back into the closed position.

Dan jumped toward the door and tried to pull back the handle.

He pulled as hard as he could. The door didn't budge. He turned to Amy, his face ashen.

"I think it's jammed. At least on this side. We're trapped."

Amy's phone buzzed again. It was another text from Jake.

Get out now!

But they couldn't get out.

And then they heard footsteps growing closer.

Isabel was almost there.

And if she found them here, they were dead.

Amy knew the woman would not miss a second time.

CHAPTER 21

Another text banged into Amy's cell phone.

Get Out Now!!!

She frantically texted back.

We're locked in!!!!

Dan picked up a bag.

"What are you doing?" she asked.

"I'm slugging the first person that comes through that door."

Amy looked quickly around the space. The room was small. No place to take cover. They couldn't hide in the bathroom. It was too tiny; she knew by the one in their compartment. And she assumed that Isabel at some point would have to use the facilities, too. Although part of Amy was not against scaring the woman half to death when she opened the door only to find Dan and herself wedged inside.

"They're coming," hissed Dan. He held the bag higher.

That's when Amy saw it. A way out.

She raced to the far corner of the room.

"Dan, look, these compartments are modular. The walls can be moved. To make bigger rooms, I guess for families traveling together."

"So what?" Dan hissed. "I don't care about families traveling together. I just don't want to die."

She ignored this and said, "That bad patch of track we passed seems to have dislodged this section of wall."

There was a small gap there.

Dan raced to her side and peered into the next compartment.

"It looks empty," he said. "They've probably gone to the dining car. But it's not wide enough for us to get through."

"We have to pull and make it bigger. Come on. Help me."

She and Dan gripped the edge of the wall and yanked as hard as they could. Amy could feel the wall moving.

Amy worked out a lot and was stronger than normal kids her age. She was glad of the extra muscle as she felt the wall give even more as it slid along the tracks on the floor.

"Hurry," said Dan. "She's almost here."

"Together, then, one-two-three."

They each gave a gigantic tug. Dan felt something pop in his shoulder but he didn't care because the wall slid another foot.

"Go, go!" said Amy.

Dan threw himself through the gap.

Amy followed right behind him.

They tumbled to the floor but were up again in an instant.

"Hurry, hurry," said Amy.

They pulled on the wall again, this time in the opposite direction.

They could hear Isabel at her door.

They pulled as hard as they could.

The wall slid and snapped into place right as they heard Isabel's door slide open with a bang and close behind her.

Amy and Dan stood there frozen, trying to catch their breath.

Dan looked at her and whispered, "What if she sees something that tells her the compartment was searched?"

Amy shook her head. "Just be ready to run."

He nodded and they stood there, listening.

They heard Isabel moving around the compartment, talking to herself.

When they heard her release a loud fart, Dan could barely keep from howling with laughter.

After a few more seconds they heard Isabel settle down in her chair right as the lights on the train came back on.

Amy slipped to the door to the compartment and peered out the window.

"Coast looks clear."

They slipped out right as an elderly couple came around the corner.

The man said, "Hey, what were you doing in our compartment?"

Thinking quickly, Dan said, "We smelled gas. We thought there might be a problem. But it's okay to go back in." He had to hide his smile as he thought of Isabel and her loud fart.

"Do you work for Amtrak?" asked the woman suspiciously. "You're not wearing uniforms."

"And you're too young, anyway," added the man accusingly.

"We're sort of trainees," said Amy. "Our uncle is the head conductor. He told us to look around for any problems after the lights went out. We're going to report to him now. Your compartment is completely safe to re-enter."

"But if you continue to smell stinky gas," said Dan, "I would check with the woman in the compartment next to yours. That might be the source."

Sniggering, he and Amy hustled off toward their compartment.

When they were out of sight of the old couple, they sprinted.

They hooked back up with Jake and Atticus, who were pacing anxiously in Dan and Amy's compartment.

When Jake saw Amy he gave her a quick hug.

"Omigosh, we didn't know what to do."

Atticus added, "Jake wanted to charge Isabel and

her men and sacrifice himself to save you, but I told him that would be both irrational and counterproductive."

Amy beamed at Jake. "You were going to do that? For me?"

"Well, yeah," said Jake, looking embarrassed.

Amy gave him another hug and a pat on the back. "Thanks, Jake. My hero."

"Hello?" said Dan heatedly. "We did get away by ourselves. So if anyone deserves a pat on the back, it's us."

"Did you find anything in Isabel's compartment that could be helpful?" asked Atticus.

Amy nodded. "We found out that Isabel was sending texts to Dan pretending to be our dad."

"I'm sorry to hear you discovered that."

They whirled around and saw her.

Isabel Kabra stood there in the doorway with her henchmen, looking triumphant.

CHAPTER 22

The large truck barreled down the road. Inside the back were the hostages, chained to the truck wall. They all felt every bump and every swerve. Some of them looked sick to their stomachs. They had been riding in the back of the truck for what seemed like days, but actually had been about fifteen hours. After one nauseating lurch, which slammed him against the side of the truck, Ted Starling threw up.

"Oh, gross," complained Natalie as she tried to move away from the pile of sick on the truck floor. "That's disgusting."

"Better get used to seeing it," said Fiske, who looked very pale indeed. "I think before this ride is over we're all going to vomit."

As they went over the top of a hill, the truck almost seemed to take flight. Several of the hostages clutched at their stomachs.

Ian said, "I think I'm going to be sick, too."

"Don't be ridiculous," said his sister. "Lucians don't get sick to their stomachs."

As the truck gave another sickening lurch, Natalie turned green and threw up. She stared down in horror at the pool of puke.

"You might want to check your Lucian status," moaned Nellie.

Nellie wasn't nauseated, but she'd been getting slammed around with the truck's movements, and her wounded shoulder had taken most of the impacts. She clutched at it with her hand, as though trying to push the pain away.

"I bet it's Cheyenne driving," complained Hamilton. "She's a psycho. She's probably deliberately hitting every pothole she can just to make us suffer."

"Of course she is," snapped Evan. "She's a Vesper. She's evil. It's what evil people do."

Reagan said, "It's cold in here. I suggest that we all run in place and do push-ups to keep warm. Plus it'll keep our energy up."

Fiske held up the shackles they all had on. "And exactly how would you like us to run, Reagan, dear, with these bloody things on?"

"That's why I said *run in place*."

"And fall over and knock ourselves out?" snapped Nellie. "I think the healthiest thing for us to do is stay still."

"And perhaps we can just all shut up, too," said Evan heatedly. He was still obviously upset about being captured.

"I can sing a song," offered Jonah. "Word."

"No!" everyone shouted in unison.

Evan eyed him threateningly. "Not one note, not one lyric, or I'll cream you."

"Why so hostile all of a sudden, bro?" asked Jonah innocently.

"Oh, I don't know, maybe being carried by a roller coaster to my death might be a reason," snapped Evan. "So just sit there and do not even hum."

Ted Starling sat in a far corner saying nothing. He was concentrating on every sound he could. He was trying to take in any information that could help him determine where they were being taken. He didn't know if it would do any good, but it wasn't like he had anything else to do right now.

Fiske pulled angrily on his shackles. Each of the hostages was tied together with the same long chain. The chain had been run through a large bolt in the wall of the truck. When Fiske pulled on the chain once more, it hit the side of the truck and dug a divot out of the wood.

Fiske stared at this divot and then said, "Listen up, everyone, I've got an idea."

"You have a song you want me to sing?" said Jonah. "We could do a duet. I'll be baritone. Just follow my lead."

"I don't have a song, you twit. I have a plan. To escape."

In the cab of the truck Cheyenne was indeed driving.

And, as Hamilton had speculated, she was attempting to hit every pothole, take every curve at top speed, and do her best to make the truck fly over every steep rise in the road.

"I'll bet they're just loving the ride back there," she said gleefully.

"Your infantile pleasure with pain and suffering is ingratiating," said Sandy, who sat next to her. Casper sat on the other side of him looking glum, principally because his sister wouldn't let him drive.

"What do you mean by that?" snapped Cheyenne.

"How much longer?" asked Casper. "I'm hungry."

"Just tell your stomach to shut up, dear brother," barked Cheyenne. "We have a schedule to keep."

"Look at that sky," Sandy said with relish.

The others eyed the sky. Clouds were going across it so fast it still looked like one of those accelerated weather maps on TV.

Sandy rubbed his hands together. "This is going to be so good. I'm going to be weatherman of the year."

"What's so great about that?" grunted Casper, who stared moodily out the window, but apparently without seeing what Sandy was referring to.

"What's great about that, Casper," began Sandy as though he were speaking to a child, "is that it has begun."

"The Doomsday device?" exclaimed Cheyenne.

"No," sneered Sandy. "The aurora borealis. Of course the Doomsday device."

"Aurora what?" said Casper, sounding confused.

"The northern lights," snapped his sister. "He was being condescending, which is really starting to get on my nerves." She looked murderously at the weatherman.

"Now, now, Cheyenne. We're all on the same team, right?" Sandy's gaze bored into her.

She said, "Of course we are."

"Excellent, because Vesper One does not tolerate disloyalty. In fact, he hates it so much the only punishment for it is immediate termination. And I don't mean losing one's job."

He looked over at Casper, who was staring at him nervously.

"You've both seen the refined ways that our peerless leader can dispose of his enemies. So, don't become his enemies. Just go along for the ride." He clapped them both on the shoulders. "And you'll have nothing to worry about. Otherwise, well, let's not dwell on such unpleasant and lethal possibilities."

Sandy closed his eyes and went to sleep while Casper and his sister shot nervous glances at each other.

The truck raced on while the sky kept doing extraordinarily odd things.

CHAPTER 23

Isabel stared directly at Amy. "So close in DC. So close. How you escaped, I still can't quite fathom. What did you tell the police?"

Dan started to say something. But Amy, sensing he was going to tell Isabel how he had fooled her, said, "We told them enough to have them more than a little interested in you. The FBI, too. For the record, they know you bought your way out of prison. They know your AWW is a fraud. And they're working very hard right now to see that you go back where you belong: prison. In fact, there are several agents on the train right now."

Isabel had been looking at her darkly. Now she laughed. "I might have believed you up to that point. There's nothing easier to spot than an FBI agent. And there are none aboard this train."

"Are you absolutely certain of that?" asked Dan smugly.

"Yes, I am." She turned to Atticus. "The last Guardian.

The truly *last* Guardian," she said menacingly.

"Yes, I am," replied Atticus quietly. "One of one. Tell me, how does it feel to be number two?"

Isabel's features turned even darker. "You should not comment on things you don't understand."

"Oh, I understand a lot. I understand that the Vespers are evil and will sell each other out to get to the top. That makes all of you weak. It's teamwork and self-sacrifice that makes winners. And that means that you Vespers are losers. And you always will be."

Isabel held out a hand and one of her guards immediately placed a syringe in it. She eyed it and took off the protective cap. "As you know, I'm singularly adept with poisons, along with my many other gifts. It's just how my mind works. My *superior* mind."

"Like your kids, Ian and Natalie? But they were smart enough to figure out you were a loser of a mother," said Dan.

Isabel held up the syringe. "This concoction is particularly nasty. Before it kills, it places the person in indescribable pain, for one hour. They will wish to die. And at the end of sixty minutes, that wish is granted."

When she advanced on Atticus, first Jake, then Amy, and lastly Dan stepped in front of her.

She said, "Oh, don't worry. Each of you will get your turn."

"Really?" said Amy. "Well, let me give you *your* turn first."

She kicked the syringe out of Isabel's hand. At the

same moment, Jake plowed into a guard, knocking the gun out of his hand.

A split second later the train roared into a tunnel. Every single light on the train, including the emergency lighting, went out. They were plunged into total darkness.

The truck continued to bounce along. In the front seat, Sandy was still sound asleep.

Casper had rolled down his window and was checking his reflection in the truck's side mirror. He looked at his sister as she steered the big vehicle.

He said, "Do I look like I'm putting on weight? My cheeks look a bit plump and my jawline doesn't seem as classical as before."

She gave him a vicious stare. "Who cares? And put the mirror back to where it was. I can't see on that side."

He grumpily did so.

As the miles piled up he checked to make sure Sandy was still sleeping and said, "So, the plan is all set for when we get there?"

Cheyenne shot a glance at Sandy, listened to his soft snores, and said, "Yes. He'll never see it coming."

Casper chuckled. "Can't wait to see the look on his face."

"Yeah."

"So cool and cruel. What could be better?"

"And you'll definitely make the top six," she said.

Casper frowned. "What happened in Switzerland wasn't my fault."

She shrugged. "You can believe that if you want."

Casper folded his arms across his chest. "You're V-Six now. You'll definitely move up."

"Yes, I will," she said sharply. "A lot higher than Six."

She glanced at Sandy, who was still snoring peacefully.

"In fact, higher than him."

"Have you heard from her?" Casper asked warily.

Cheyenne shook her head and motioned to Sandy, who was now moving around a bit before settling back in his seat.

Neither one of them noticed that when Sandy had moved, he had adjusted the volume on the recorder hidden in his pocket. He smiled inwardly. He had always been so good at feigning sleep. It was a useful skill, now paying huge dividends.

In the rear of the truck, Fiske was urging the others on.

All the hostages were slapping the side of the truck where the bolt was located with their length of chain. The floor was littered with wood and composite chips carved out of the truck wall by their energetic thrusts.

Fiske said, "Keep going. We're almost there. Once we work the bolt out of the wall, we're free."

Jonah, who was wearily hitting his section of chain

against the wall, said, "Free? Bro, we're still locked in a truck."

"True," said Fiske. "But now we're chained up in a locked truck. When we're no longer chained and they have to open the truck to let us out, the truck is no longer locked. Get it?"

"Got it." Jonah started whacking the wall with renewed energy.

Even Nellie, with her wounded shoulder, was taking her turn with the wall. She grimaced every time she hit the wall with her part of the chain, but she doggedly kept going.

Hamilton and Reagan were the most aggressive of all. They were slamming their chains against the side of the wall so hard it seemed like they were in danger of knocking the truck over on its side.

Fiske finally grabbed Hamilton and said, "Appreciate the max effort, son, but we are trying to do this somewhat on the sly."

A sweaty-faced Hamilton said, "Oh, right. Sure."

They proceeded, but at a somewhat moderated pace.

Fiske stepped back and studied the loosening bolt and then the rear door of the truck. It was locked, that he knew. He had heard the lock slide into place when Casper had lowered the overhead door.

He ran his gaze along the distance between the bolt and the door. He made some calculations in his head. Things might come together nicely. He was very much looking forward to knocking Casper Wyoming right on

DAY OF DOOM

his butt. He figured he could just run Cheyenne over with the truck. Sandy he would string up to the tallest pole he could find, wrapped with metal, and let a stray bolt of lightning finish him off. These thoughts made him smile.

And they also gave him hope. And energy.

He picked up his length of chain and began gouging at the wood.

Nellie looked at him and smiled weakly.

"Do you think we have a chance?" she asked.

He smiled grimly back at her. "I'll let you know as soon as we get this bolt out. When we do, then I think it's time for something."

"Time? Time for what?"

"Payback," said Fiske grimly.

He and Nellie beat the sides of the wall harder than ever.

Then Fiske suddenly stopped and listened.

"Quiet, everyone. Stop what you're doing."

They all froze and stared at him.

Fiske listened more closely.

Ted Starling had sensed it before anyone else.

"We're slowing down," he said. "I think we're almost at our destination."

Fiske roared, "Go! Go! As hard as you can. Do it."

They all started smashing the wall as hard as they could. The bolt started to come out of the wall.

The truck started slowing down more.

"Go! GO!" shouted Fiske.

Hamilton reared back and gave the bolt one more mighty whack.

It fell to the floor.

They all looked at one another.

"We're free," gasped Nellie.

"Not quite," said Fiske.

The truck had stopped abruptly, throwing them all forward.

"Now what?" asked Ian fearfully.

They all heard it.

Doors opening and then thumping closed.

"They're coming," hissed Natalie as she drew back from the door.

"What do we do?" Nellie asked, looking at Fiske.

Fiske took charge. "Listen to me and listen very carefully. We only have one shot to get this right."

They all drew around as he began to explain their plan of attack.

CHAPTER 24

In the darkness, bodies flew around and crashed into walls, furniture, and one another. There was a lot of yelling, groaning, and panting as the fighting continued.

Dan took a fist to the head and yelled out.

"Sorry," said Jake, and he swung his fist the other way and knocked one of Isabel's guards into the window. The man slid down, stunned.

Amy was kicking and lashing out at anyone who came near her. Her foot collided with someone's stomach, and she was gratified to hear Isabel gasp. She kicked out even harder, but Isabel was no longer there.

The shot rang out so loud that everyone stopped fighting.

Dan instinctively ducked and rolled to his left. On the floor he spotted Amy and Jake, on either side of him.

Amy said, "Are you hit?"

"No," replied Dan.

"Jake?" she said frantically. "Are you hit?"

"No."

They heard something hit the floor.

"That doesn't sound good," whispered Dan.

Ten long seconds passed.

Then the lights came back on.

Amy, Dan, and Jake jumped up, ready to continue fighting.

There was no one left to fight.

But there was someone still there.

One of Isabel's henchmen.

His coat was bloody. His face was gray. He was not breathing.

"Omigosh," exclaimed Amy.

She dropped to the floor and checked his pulse.

She looked up.

"He's dead."

This did not come from Amy.

They all glanced at the doorway as Sinead stepped into the opening with a gun in hand.

Amy said furiously, "You killed him!"

"Before he shot you."

"It was dark; how could he see to shoot?" countered Amy.

Dan piped in, "And you're the one with the gun."

To their amazement Sinead put the gun down, came in the compartment, and shut the door.

"Look more closely at him," she said.

They did.

Dan was the first to spot it. "Hey, he's wearing glasses."

"Not just any glasses," said Sinead. "Pick them up."

Dan did so. He put them on. "They're night-vision goggles."

"I wrestled the pistol away from him right before he was about to shoot you, Amy. It went off while we were fighting. I actually didn't mean to shoot him."

Jake picked up the gun and looked at Amy. "She's telling the truth. This was the gun the guy was holding. I saw it when he was next to Isabel."

"But why?" Amy asked Sinead. "Why would you help me?"

"I won't lie and say it's because I love you, because I don't."

"Yeah, that I get. You tried to kill me, after all, using your little gun. And you would have if I hadn't knocked it out of your hand."

"All true. Although I really didn't want to kill you back then. And I don't want to kill you now."

"Right," snorted Dan. "And I'm actually Harry Potter, only I've misplaced my wand, lightning scar, and glasses."

"So why?" Amy asked again.

"I love my brothers. That's why I've done all the terrible things I've done."

"What does that have to do with us?" asked Amy. "We've been trying to rescue Ted and the other hostages."

Dan snapped, "And you helped them get kidnapped."

Sinead said, "I knew they were going to be kidnapped, it's true. But I didn't help them do it. It was a way to provide me with an alibi in case you got suspicious of me."

"But Ned got away," pointed out Dan.

"That was his own doing. Vesper One promised me that he wouldn't hurt Ted."

Amy said, "And you believed him?"

Dan added, "If you did, you should have your head examined."

"I *did* believe him. Until he sent those pictures of the hostages. I know that Alistair is dead. And the others looked so . . . so hurt. Including Ted. I begged him to let him go, but he wouldn't."

"Coulda told you that a long time ago," barked Dan.

"So, why are you here?" asked Amy.

"I have no other choice," said Sinead, looking miserable. "I have no other place to turn. Ted is not doing well as a captive. And Vesper One has made it quite clear that he will not be releasing Ted. He says he knows too much."

"Nice little communication you've been having with old Vesper One," said Jake in disgust.

Sinead looked at him. "I don't blame you for not understanding why I've done what I have. But let me be clear. I'm not looking for your forgiveness, either." She directed this last comment at Amy. Then she eyed Dan again. "Do you have the serum? I was around you long enough to know that you had a heightened interest in it. And your little excursions? Those were to get the necessary ingredients, right?"

Dan involuntarily looked over at his knapsack and caught a breath.

It was gone.

Then Jake screamed, "Atticus! Where is Atticus?"

They all looked around. In all the confusion they hadn't realized Atticus was no longer there.

Amy said, "Isabel must have him. And she took your knapsack, too, Dan."

Sinead said, "As I was struggling with the guy, I felt people rushing past me and out into the corridor."

Jake looked sick. "I was just standing here and didn't even realize my brother was missing? What kind of older brother am I?" he added miserably.

He suddenly snatched up the gun and rushed out of the compartment yelling for Atticus.

"Jake, wait," cried Amy, but he had already disappeared down the corridor.

She turned to look at Dan and Sinead. "They must still be on the train. We just have to find them."

"What about him?" asked Dan, pointing down at the dead man.

Amy said, "There's nothing we can do for him."

Sinead added, "He deserved what he got."

Amy eyed her severely. "That applies to you, too." She turned to Dan. "The serum? Was it in your bag?"

He looked at her but said nothing. He could see

Sinead waiting for his answer.

Amy said again, "*Do* you have the serum? The real stuff?"

Dan said, "Yes. It was in my bag."

"Meaning Isabel has it now," said Sinead. "Great." She looked down at the man's body and then listened for a moment to footsteps heading their way.

"Unless we want to waste time explaining why a dead body is in your compartment, I suggest that we get out of here. Now."

Amy, Dan, and Sinead ran out of the compartment and headed away from the sounds of the onrushing feet and in the direction Jake had run.

As they were running, Amy whispered to Dan, "How did Isabel know you had the serum?"

Dan shrugged but then an idea hit him. "As she was pretending to send me texts as Dad, I . . . I might have mentioned something about the serum."

"Might have or did?"

"Okay, did."

"Because she asked you about it?"

"Yeah," Dan admitted. "She really conned me."

"She's good at that, Dan. After all, she's conned millions of people."

They were suddenly hurtled forward and slammed into Sinead. All three went down in a tangle of limbs.

"Get off me!" wheezed Sinead. "You're on my stomach. I can't breathe."

"What happened?" said Dan as he rolled off her.

"The train just slammed to a stop," explained Amy.

"That I get. But why?" snapped Sinead.

"Trains usually stop when someone wants to get off," replied Amy.

They all stood and Dan glanced out the window. "But we're still in the tunnel. Who would want to get off in a tunnel?"

The train lights suddenly went out. They were once more standing in the pitch black.

"I can think of one person who might want to get off," said Amy.

"Isabel," added Sinead.

"And if she's getting off, so are we," said Amy.

"How?" asked Dan. "I can't see a thing."

"But I can," said Amy.

"How?" asked Dan again.

"I took the man's night-vision goggles. Dan, hold on to my hand. Sinead, take ahold of Dan's shirt. Now let's go. That woman is not getting away with Atticus."

CHAPTER 25

As they were trying to get off the train they heard an announcement over the repaired PA.

"Ladies and gentlemen, we're experiencing some difficulties with our power system. Please remain where you are while our crew addresses the problem. We should be up and running shortly. Thank you for your patience, and thank you for choosing Amtrak for your travel needs."

"Right," grumbled Dan. "Never again."

"Amy?" The voice came at them from out of the darkness.

"Jake?"

Amy focused her goggles a bit better and saw Jake at the end of the corridor. He still had the gun in his hand. They hurried forward to join him.

"Jake, what happened? Did you find Atticus?"

"No," he said miserably. "I lost them."

The lights came back on and Amy took off her goggles.

She said, "If Isabel got off the train, we need to as well."

Jake said, "We're in a tunnel. Why would she get off here?"

"I don't know. But I can't believe that the train just happened to come to a stop here for no reason. She has to be behind it."

"I was listening for any exterior door to open," said Jake. "I didn't hear any. And if there's no power, can they even get the doors open?"

"There must be a way to do that in an emergency," Sinead pointed out.

Dan piped in, "Look, we don't know enough, okay? We're just grasping at straws here. We need more information. Like, why would Isabel want to be getting off at the Rocky Mountains in Colorado? Because that's where we are. I checked the schedule. The Cascade Mountains are a long way from here." Even as he said it, Dan looked puzzled, as though a curious thought had just occurred to him.

Sinead said, "Dan's right. Maybe the train really has broken down."

"Who cares?" exclaimed Jake. "We need to get Atticus back. He's the last Guardian. She's going to kill him."

Dan looked to his right. "Hey, isn't that your compartment, Jake?"

"I doubt Atticus is in there," he barked.

"But your laptop is. Let's get online and try to figure this out."

"How will going online get Atticus back?" snapped Jake.

In response Dan pulled his phone out of his pocket and brought up the photos of the Lewis and Clark compass he'd taken in DC. "Before everything happened, I was studying this."

"Why?" asked Amy. "We already know what it says about the latitude and longitude."

"Do we?" said Dan. "Do we really? I'm not so sure. I think we missed something. Something potentially big. And we know Isabel was really interested in the compass. She wouldn't have gone to all that trouble for nothing. There has to be something important about it."

Jake said, "We know that. It told her the coordinates for the Cascades."

"Maybe, maybe not," said Dan mysteriously.

Amy looked at Jake. "I guess it won't hurt to take a few minutes to look at this. And it might help us figure out where they might be taking Atticus."

Sinead added, "And you running around the train holding a gun will just get you arrested, Jake. That certainly won't help Atticus."

Jake looked down at the gun in his hand, engaged the safety, and then stuck it in his waistband and covered it with his shirt. "Okay, but let's hurry."

They went inside the compartment and Jake fired up his laptop.

Amy said, "If the train starts back up again, we all need to make a decision whether to stay on or get off."

"How can we make that decision?" asked Sinead. "If we get off and Isabel didn't, we're stuck inside a mountain."

Jake said bitterly, "Yeah, but if we don't get off and Isabel does with Atticus, we'll never see him again. So we're stuck between a rock and a hard place inside a mountain. No stupid pun intended."

Dan said, "Which makes it all the more important to get more information. We can't stop Isabel or Vesper One, and get Atticus and the hostages back, without knowing more."

Jake was clicking keys on his laptop. "Okay, I'm connected to the web. Now what?"

"Let me have your phone. The picture you took of the back of the compass is better than the shot I took."

Jake dug into his pocket and tossed Dan his phone.

Dan quickly brought the photo up on the screen. He enlarged it and studied the markings on the back they had gone over before.

Sinead said, "Anything?"

Dan shook his head. "I still can't quite make it out." He shot Amy a glance. "Wait a minute. Those night-vision goggles you took. They can magnify things."

"Yeah, when it's dark. But it's not dark, in case you hadn't noticed," said Sinead.

Amy said, "But we can make it dark. Quick, turn out all the lights in here. Jake, close your laptop."

They turned off all the lights, drew the door and window curtains closed, and Jake quickly pushed down the cover of his laptop, shutting off the screen light.

Dan put on the goggles and fired them up. He leaned down close to the photo.

"Okay, I'm seeing something. Too bad the res on the picture isn't better."

"That's the best a cell-phone camera can do," barked Jake. "And if you don't come up with something in, like, five seconds, I'm going to go look for Att with or without you."

Dan adjusted the magnification on the goggles. "Oh, wow, that's better. Okay, let me see."

Sinead, who had not been with them in DC and did not know what any of this represented, hissed, "Why is this important? We're wasting time."

"No, we're not wasting time," Dan shot back. "I think we're about to make a huge breakthrough."

He adjusted the magnification on the goggles again, revving them up to full power. He leaned as close as he could to the phone screen.

"Okay, we looked at these before and came up with the latitude and longitude coordinates for the Cascade Mountain Range."

"Right," said Amy. "Latitude forty-seven degrees north and longitude one hundred and twenty-one degrees west."

"Hey, wait just a minute," exclaimed Dan. " Someone has messed with these numbers. I can see it clearly with the goggles. I don't think that seven is really a seven. A line was scratched out. I think it's really a zero. And the one twenty-one number has been changed, too. The two and the second one have been altered. I think they were originally a zero and a six. And even from the photo it looks recently done." He squinted. "Maybe someone used, like, a stain or dark paint to cover up part of the six and zero."

"Recently done?" exclaimed Jake. "How is that possible? That compass is over two hundred years old. It's probably been in that museum for decades."

Amy snapped her fingers. "Remember the woman back at the museum?"

"Dr. Nancy Gwinn?" said Jake. "The curator who showed Isabel the compass?"

"Exactly."

"So that's why you're interested in it," said Sinead. "Because Isabel was."

"Right," said Amy. "Anyway, Gwinn said that there was almost a disaster."

Dan cried out, "She said Isabel dropped the compass and it bounced under a display cabinet."

Jake took up the story. "And Isabel got under the cabinet to get it. She would have been out of sight of Gwinn at that point."

Amy added, "And she could have used a knife or even her grotesquely long fingernails to cut into the back of the compass box, altering the numbers, then brushed off the wood shavings, and handed it back. And she might have had some stain with her that she applied to change some of the numbers. It would have only taken a few seconds. The markings were so slight to begin with Gwinn probably never even noticed the change. She was probably just happy the glass on the compass hadn't broken."

Sinead said, "But what is so important about the numbers?"

Dan said, "They showed that the perfect location

for the Doomsday device was the Cascade Mountains. But if you take away the alterations that Isabel did, the longitude becomes one hundred and six degrees west."

Amy said, "And the latitude would be forty degrees north, right?"

"Right," said Dan. He took off the goggles and they turned the compartment lights back on.

All eyes turned to Jake, who had opened up his laptop once more.

Amy said, "So, where are those coordinates?"

"Give me one sec," replied Jake, his fingers flying over the keys.

He stopped typing and stared at the screen, a confused look on his face.

"What is it, Jake?" exclaimed Amy. "Where are those coordinates?"

He looked up. "It's the Rocky Mountains. And I used a geo-locator tagged to our position." He paused. "That spot is exactly where we are right now."

CHAPTER 26

They all stared at one another.

"Here?" asked Amy. "Right where we are? How is that possible?"

Dan said, "But what about subduction zones? Wasn't that the whole point?"

Jake looked at his laptop. "That's right. That doesn't make sense. The subduction zones make the power of the Doomsday device immeasurably greater."

"Then there has to be something that we're missing," said Amy.

The PA system came on. A voice said, "Thank you for your patience. We will be moving very soon."

"Well, we don't have much time to figure it out," warned Sinead.

She sat down next to Jake and started hitting keys on the laptop.

"What are you doing?" asked Jake.

"Trying to make sense of the inexplicable," she shot back. "If subduction zones are important, then we need to understand what this area has that the Cascade Mountains don't."

Her fingers flew over the keys, bringing up screen after screen.

As Amy watched her she was reminded that Sinead was unbelievably intelligent and her computer skills were second to none.

But can I trust her? wondered Amy. Her answer was automatic.

No, I can't.

Sinead stopped clicking keys and looked up.

"I think I've got it."

Jake studied the screen and Amy and Dan drew closer.

Sinead said, "Apparently, there's a geological quirk in the composition of the bedrock underneath the Rocky Mountains. These mountains sit over a vast subduction zone. From what I've been able to find out in the last few minutes, that zone makes the Cascades look paltry by comparison. And because the Rockies are approximately in the middle of the country, any disruption of that zone could be potentially devastating to the entire country, not just the western part. One zone runs out due west and the other runs out due east."

Amy studied the images on the laptop's screen. "They look like underground rivers," she said.

"That's pretty much what they are," said Sinead,

and Jake nodded in agreement. "You start the power source at one end and the ramifications are felt at the other. Like a tsunami building and then crashing in a far-off place."

Amy said, "So this spot really is the perfect place for the Doomsday device?"

Dan added, "It sounds like it's subduction zone heaven."

"That's exactly right," said Sinead.

Jake said, "And that was why Isabel altered the compass numbers on the back of the Lewis and Clark box. Just in case we found out and were trying to locate that heading?"

"And it almost worked," said Sinead. She looked at Dan. "If Dan hadn't insisted on taking another look at it with those goggles, we'd be clueless."

Dan said, "Well, I was just being my typically brilliant self." He added, "But if you're trying to get on my good side by pointing out my obvious genius, it won't work. You've done too many bad things."

Sinead glanced away, her features dark.

Jake rose and slipped his laptop in his bag.

"Okay, we have to get off here. That's why the train stopped. Isabel *is* getting off. And she has Att with her."

It was merely a speck in the sky. But it soon came into sharper focus.

The lightweight experimental aircraft was flying at barely two thousand feet off the ground. Its speed was approximately 120 knots. It looked like a helicopter, only with wings.

The single pilot looked through the egg-shaped glass covering him.

Damien Vesper smiled as the terrain flew beneath him and the skies overhead crackled with unusual power. Though the winds were buffeting the aircraft and coming at odd angles, and lightning cracked upward, and the sky still looked purple, Damien piloted his aircraft with a practiced hand. He was not scared by the daunting elements; he was enjoying the show!

This was the time he had spent his whole life preparing for.

The Doomsday device was in place and partially active. He looked down at the small box that rested at his feet. Inside there was the last piece of the puzzle. It was the Madrigal ring that was actually a gear. Once he placed that on his device and cranked it to full power, the world would understand what it truly meant to fear.

His phone buzzed. He pressed a button and put on headphones.

Sandy Bancroft's recording spilled into his ears.

He listened to the Wyoming idiots plotting against him. He was not surprised. They were utterly lacking in what it took to be true leaders. They had served their purposes. Now they were expendable. He would deal with them shortly.

A while later he landed his aircraft in a field where a black SUV was waiting to pick him up. Up ahead of him soared the mighty Rockies.

From here it would all begin. His master plan had finally come to fruition. His ancestors would be so proud. But of all the Vespers that had come before, he was the only one who had actually succeeded.

The box stowed safely in his bag, Damien climbed into the SUV and was immediately driven off.

One more piece. Archimedes' precious gear.

And then it all could truly begin.

And end.

Spectacularly.

CHAPTER 27

Cheyenne had driven the truck into a vast chamber that had been carved into the mountain. A large overhead door had opened and closed automatically as the truck approached.

Cheyenne, Sandy, and Casper climbed out of the truck cab and headed for the rear of the truck.

"Let's hurry up," Sandy ordered Casper and Cheyenne.

Cheyenne glared at him. "Who died and made you boss?"

"In case you forgot, Cheyenne, in the Vesper pecking order, I rank above you." Sandy gazed at Casper. "And you're not even in that pecking order."

"Yeah, well, pecking orders can change!" snapped Casper.

"Maybe in your fantasy world," replied Sandy. "Your problem is you're not content to just be a follower. But your abilities are perfectly suited to such a status."

Cheyenne said, "Hey, Casper, I think he just insulted you."

Casper balled up a large fist and said to Sandy, "You're a fancy-pants weather guy, right? Predict stuff?"

"I prefer 'world-class meteorologist,' but let's not quibble over titles. Yes, I predict things."

Casper popped him in the face. "So how come you didn't see that coming?"

Sandy held his bloody nose while Cheyenne laughed.

"Open the truck door," yelled Sandy between his fingers. "Now!"

"Sure thing, *boss*," snorted Casper.

He unlocked the padlock and pushed up the truck door.

"AAAAGGGHHH!"

The hostages, led by Hamilton, Evan, Reagan, and Fiske, leaped out, still chained together, and fell on top of Sandy, Cheyenne, and Casper.

When Casper stood and started swinging, Reagan leveled him with a wicked spin kick.

"Sweet," exclaimed Reagan as Casper crashed to the floor. "Been wanting to try out that move, doofus."

Cheyenne jumped to her feet and caught Evan with a jab and an uppercut. He went down, but Hamilton slammed into Cheyenne and sent her flying against the wall. She hit it and slid down, unconscious. Hamilton towered over her and flexed his biceps.

"Man, that felt good," he said. "What I live for. Winning and creaming people."

Casper got back up only to be leveled by a right cross

and vicious uppercut thrown by Fiske Cahill.

As Casper collapsed backward, unconscious, Fiske said, "Been wanting payback since that little thrashing you gave me in Switzerland, you punk."

Sandy got to his feet and ran, but Fiske, using his wrapped chain as a lasso, tossed it around Sandy's neck and jerked him backward.

"Haven't finished with you yet, old boy," said Fiske. "It's been a while since I had the opportunity to pummel someone closer to my own age."

Sandy turned to him, gurgling, his eyes popping as he gripped the chain.

"What's that you say?" asked Fiske mockingly. "Oh, you want me to hit you very hard in the mouth? Delighted."

Fiske slammed his fist into Sandy's face and the world-class (in his own mind) meteorologist slumped to the ground, knocked out cold.

"We need a key!" called out Nellie, who had been flung all over the place while the others were fighting. She held her injured shoulder and was trying hard not to scream in pain.

Hamilton dug into Cheyenne's jacket pocket and held up the key to the shackles.

"Got it."

"Someone's coming," warned Ted, who'd been listening intently for this very thing.

"Quick," said Fiske. "Out this way. We can unlock the chains later."

He looked down once more at Sandy and gave him an extra kick in the side.

"That's for Alistair, you evil little man!"

They rushed through a doorway and entered a rock tunnel. To the left, they heard the sounds of people approaching. Still all chained together, they headed to the right with Hamilton in the lead. He was so tall and his strides so long that some of the shorter people fell to the floor.

"Let's get in sync," said Reagan. "Or we'll just be captured again. Come on, one-two, one-two, one-two. Left-right, left-right."

They left the tunnel, turned right, and kept going. Once they could no longer hear the sounds of people rushing down the tunnels, they stopped and Hamilton unlocked the chains with the key he'd taken from Cheyenne.

They all looked around while they caught their breath.

"Where are we?" asked Nellie.

The other nine hostages, suddenly free, but far from safe, looked at one another.

"Feels like we're inside a mountain," noted Ian.

His sister nodded. "It's so cold and dark."

"But not completely dark," observed Fiske. "There are low-level lights throughout these tunnels. That is not naturally occurring. There must be some source of power, possibly a generator."

"But who would have a generator inside a mountain?" asked Evan.

Fiske looked at Phoenix. "Phoenix, you got away before. Where were we?"

"In Washington State," answered Phoenix. "Somewhere in the Cascade Mountains."

"So why move us from those mountains to wherever we are now, inside another mountain?" wondered Nellie.

Ted said, "I think we're somewhere in the Rockies."

They all looked at him.

"How can you know that?" asked Hamilton skeptically.

"I counted the seconds in the trip. And one of the wheels on the truck had an imperfection. I could feel and hear the resulting bump and squeak. I calculated the revolutions of the wheels and arrived at the approximate speed we were being driven. Multiplying that by the length of the trip equaled roughly thirteen hundred miles. That's about the distance between Seattle and Denver, give or take. That is if we were heading east. But heading south in that direction would not really put us in a mountain range. And north would be in Canada with the same issue."

"But why hold us in the Cascades and then move us to the Rockies?" asked a bewildered Jonah. "It makes no sense."

"It obviously makes sense to someone."

"Someone like Vesper One," said Nellie grimly.

Fiske took charge. "All right. We have gained our freedom, but we're still in great danger. They'll know by now that we have escaped. They will be searching for us. They will know the layout of these tunnels better than we do. I think the best strategy is to split up. That way if we are captured, they won't get us all, at least in one fell swoop."

"Sounds like a plan we can execute," said Reagan in her pumped-up, kick-butt Reagan way. "So let's divvy up the assets and go nail some Vespers."

Fiske looked them all over. "Okay, there are ten of us, so we'll go five and five. I'll lead one group. Ian, you take the other."

Reagan looked incredulous. "You didn't pick *me* as a leader?"

Fiske smiled sweetly. "Dear Reagan, I know your propensity to fight, as well as your brother's, and your desire to be at the forefront of the action. But the leader must stay back, not be captured or hurt. I didn't want either of you to have to work against your own very natural instincts."

Reagan brightened at this explanation. "Okay, then. Good thinking."

"Yeah," added Hamilton. He smacked his fist into his palm. "I am definitely ready to bust some Vesper heads."

Fiske split them into groups. He took Nellie, Reagan, Jonah, and Ted with him. That left Hamilton, Evan, Phoenix, and Natalie to go with Ian.

Before they headed out in separate directions Fiske said, "Whatever happens, I want you to know how very proud I am of all of you. The bravery you've shown. No person could ever have any people better than you in a dangerous situation. It has been my honor to serve with you."

Some of them blinked back tears. Even Reagan and Hamilton looked misty-eyed.

Fiske continued, "This will not be easy. It will be very difficult, in fact. Whatever the Vespers are planning, it will not be good for the world. We must do all we can to save it. Even if we have to die for it."

Fiske looked at them all. "Good luck."

The two groups set off in opposite directions to save the world.

CHAPTER 28

"Ready?" Jake asked the others.

Amy stared resolutely back at him. "Ready."

Jake pushed the button to open the door of the train car they were in.

The door hissed open and Jake looked out.

"Pretty dark tunnel," he said.

Dan exclaimed, "What did you expect, big guy, bright, shiny lights pointing to exactly where we need to go?"

"Shut up, Dan," said Amy crossly.

They climbed off the train and reached the track bed. Only a few feet separated the train car from the side of the tunnel.

"Keep tight to the wall," said Jake.

"Which way do we go?" asked Amy.

Before Jake could answer, they saw a pinpoint of light farther down to their right.

"Get down," hissed Jake, and they quickly knelt.

"What is it?" whispered Sinead.

Amy slapped on the night-vision goggles and focused them.

"It's Isabel and her people. And they have Atticus."

"At least he's still alive," said Jake grimly.

"And at least we know which way to go," said Amy. "We just follow them."

"And get Atticus back," said Dan.

"Safely," added Jake.

"Okay, we can start moving," said Amy. "They've gone far enough ahead. Just keep quiet."

They moved forward and then stopped.

Dan said anxiously, "Was that just me, or is the mountain shaking?"

"The mountain is definitely shaking," said Amy. "Let's pick up the pace a little."

They hurried along faster. Amy was in the lead because she had on the goggles and could see the best.

She hissed, "It looks like they're stopping. No, wait a minute. I think they're going through a door."

"A door!" exclaimed Sinead. "In the mountain?"

"Well, there's a tunnel in the mountain, so it makes sense that there might be rooms carved in here, too, like for train supplies and emergency equipment and stuff," noted Dan.

"Let's hurry," said Amy.

They picked up their pace even more.

Then another sound reached their ears.

Jake said nervously, "Um, is the train starting to move?"

They all glanced at the long double-decker train that was next to them. It was definitely starting to move. The big metal wheels were turning.

"Hurry!" said Amy.

They ran headlong toward the door that Isabel and the others had already gone through.

The train started to move faster. They could feel the force of the airflow created by the moving train start to pull them toward it.

"Once it starts going fast enough, it'll create enormous suction," cried out Dan. "Especially in a tunnel. It'll be strong enough to throw us right under the wheels."

"Faster," shouted Amy. "Run."

They sprinted as fast as they could. But they were also running in the same direction the train was going, so they would never be able to reach the end of the train where the air pressure created by the train's speed would no longer exist.

"It's really moving now," shouted Jake as he ran after Amy.

Dan could feel the force of the airflow being pushed along by the train. He could almost feel his heels starting to be lifted off the ground.

They reached the door, but the shallow doorway cut in the solid rock provided almost no relief from the building air pressure.

Amy stared at the door in dismay.

"It's a combo lock," she said. "We don't have the code," she added quite unnecessarily. The light on the alarm box glowed red. It might as well have said "KEEP OUT AND DIE!" in Amy's mind, because if they couldn't get through the door they were dead.

"Let me see it," snapped Sinead, and she pushed Amy out of the way.

It was a pad with buttons and an LED screen.

Sinead pulled a can of something from her bag.

"What's that?" asked Dan.

"A chemical that causes material to fluoresce in the darkness," she answered. "I carry it with me in case I need to get in somewhere."

"And how exactly does that help us?" asked Dan.

The train was moving faster and faster. They now had to hold on to one another to keep from being sucked under the wheels. But soon, that would no longer be enough.

"Just watch," said Sinead.

"We're going to, like, die, guys, real soon," yelled Jake.

Sinead sprayed the pad. Four number keys glowed with Isabel's fingerprints, where she had touched them.

"Okay, it's a four-digit code," said Sinead. "Now we just need the correct order to make the door open. For that we need some number-crunching capability."

Jake, seeing where she was going with this, pulled out his laptop. He fired it up.

"Do you have a USB cable?" shouted Sinead. "We can interface with the lock's computer that way. There's a port on the side."

He pulled one from his pocket and popped the USB cable into the side of the laptop and handed the other end to Sinead.

Sinead plugged the cord into the port on the side of the locking mechanism.

Jake brought up an app on his computer and hit the start button on the program.

The train was reaching its top speed. Amy grabbed hold of Dan, who was the closest to the train tracks. He was literally being lifted off his feet. Amy held on to him with one hand and grabbed the door handle with the other.

Jake leaned against the door and braced himself.

Sinead sat on her butt, and put her back against one edge of the doorway and her feet against the other, wedging herself in.

"Hurry, Jake," screamed Amy. "I can't hold on much longer."

Dan was now completely in the air and horizontal, his feet bare inches from the train whooshing by.

"How long is this freaking train?" he yelled. But no one could hear him. The train was like a tornado going by.

Amy could feel her grip slipping on her brother's wrist. She thought quickly, did the splits with her legs, and pressed one foot against one edge of the doorway directly above Sinead's head and the other foot against the other doorway edge. She leaned against Jake, who was directly in front of her. She reached back and grabbed Dan with both hands. But she felt herself being inexorably drawn toward the train.

Dan could sense this and screamed, "Let me go or you'll be sucked away, too."

Tears falling down her face, Amy shook her head stubbornly. "No!"

"Let me go."

She shook her head again. "Never," she said. "We *both* go or not at all."

Sinead reached up and snagged Amy's belt and held on for dear life.

Amy looked down and saw this. She smiled grimly at Sinead, who managed a weak smile back.

Sinead mouthed the words, *I won't let you go, Amy.*

Amy looked at her, conflicting emotions running through her head. She would have to figure that out later. For now, she focused everything on holding on to her brother.

Jake stared dead at the screen as the numbers continued to flash by.

"Come on. Come on!" he yelled.

He could feel himself being pulled backward. He pushed harder against Amy, who was holding on to Dan. Sinead was below them and holding on to

Amy. Sinead reached her other hand out and grabbed Jake's leg.

"Got it!" he yelled.

The correct order of numbers flashed across the LED screen. The red light turned to green and the door clicked open.

But the sudden opening of the door caused a powerful tunnel of wind to bleed off and into the opening behind the door.

As the massive train reached top speed, Amy, Dan, Sinead, and Jake were blown through the opening, like a mighty wave was washing them to shore.

They tumbled down the hall and landed in a heap twenty feet farther down.

"Whoa!" said Dan. He suddenly felt himself being pulled back toward the open doorway.

"It's a vacuum," cried out Amy. "It's sucking us back."

All four of them were being dragged toward the opening. The train was still flying past. They would be pulled right under it.

Ordinarily the door should have been pulled shut by the vacuum, but there was a magnetic latch holding it to the wall. Dan was the closest to the doorway, and he was clawing and fighting to hold himself away.

"This sucks like you would not believe," he cried out. "It's like a Dyson vacuum from Chernobyl."

Amy took in all that was happening. She saw that Dan was going to get pulled back out first. She also knew that once the train passed by, the vacuum action would mostly cease. But by then it would be too late for Dan. Thinking quickly, Amy stopped fighting against the vacuum, drew a long breath, and actually hurled herself toward the door opening. The vacuum grabbed her fully and she sailed over and past Dan.

Jake screamed, "Amy, no!"

As Dan watched his sister fly over, he reached up for her, but missed. "Amy, don't!" he yelled.

But Amy didn't hear Jake or her brother. Her total focus was on that doorway. Or rather, on the door. Timing would be everything.

She braced herself.

Five . . . four . . . three . . . two . . .

At the last possible instant she managed to twist her body sideways and her foot reached out and caught the edge of the door. She kicked with all her might, broke the magnetic lock, and the door closed and relocked itself.

The next instant, Amy slammed headfirst into the closed door and fell to the floor.

The vacuum had stopped as soon as the door had shut and sealed itself.

The others stood up, checking for injury.

Dan said, "Amy, that was so stupid. But you did save us."

Sinead was looking at where Amy still lay on the floor. "Amy?"

Jake, no doubt sensing the panic in her voice, looked that way, too.

"Amy!"

She was not moving. She was lying completely still, facedown. And there was blood all over.

They ran toward her as fast as they could.

CHAPTER 29

"This way," called out Fiske.

They had been moving down passageways for the last twenty minutes. Fiske had been searching for a way out at first, but realized that his best bet was to try to find some of the Vespers. If they could overpower them, they not only would have a decent shot at discovering what deadly plan the Vespers had, but also an exit. Otherwise, he was afraid they could wander in this maze for years.

The five former hostages moved down the hall as quietly as possible.

Fiske knew that if a fight took place he could count on Reagan to more than hold her own. The Tomas branch had its share of muscle, endurance, and athleticism. And Jonah, he supposed, could start singing. That might actually scare the Vespers off. Fiske knew that Jonah was an international superstar, but Fiske was not his core audience, meaning he was older than thirteen and not a girl.

However, in a fight, Ted would be helpless. And

the same was true for the injured Nellie.

Fiske thought, *Well, old boy, you're just going to have to pick up the slack.*

They came to a pentagon-shaped room that had five tunnels, including the one they were in, bleeding off from it. Fiske stopped and the others halted behind him.

"Which way?" asked Reagan.

Nellie studied the different options. "They all look the same."

"But no doubt where they lead will *not* be the same," noted Fiske.

"Should we split up further?" asked Jonah. "There are four possibilities and five of us?"

Fiske considered this for a moment but then shook his head after glancing at Nellie and Ted.

"We've diluted our numbers enough. We stick together."

"So do we eenie-meenie-miney-mo it?" asked Nellie in frustration.

"Might be as good as anything," answered Fiske.

He performed the exercise and ended with the tunnel to their immediate left.

"Let's go, troops," he said with far more confidence than he actually was feeling.

They headed down this passageway for what seemed like miles, although by Fiske's calculation it was only about twenty-four feet.

"I think I see a brighter light up there," said Reagan.

Fiske had seen it, too.

"Okay," he began in a low voice. "This may be the moment of truth. If there are Vespers in that room ahead, then we need to be prepared to fight. Reagan and I will lead the way. Jonah, your job is to protect Nellie and Ted."

Reagan said, "I thought you said leaders stayed back from the fight?"

"A little white lie," replied Fiske. "Sorry."

"And I don't need song-boy to protect me," Nellie said indignantly. "I can fight."

"Not with a wounded shoulder," pointed out Reagan.

"I've still got one good arm and two good legs," she said stubbornly.

"And I can fight, too," said Ted.

Fiske looked at him, but said nothing. However, he was thinking, *Dear boy, you can barely see.*

"All right," he said. "I'm sure we'll all encounter some action. But let's keep quiet so surprise will be on our side."

They moved forward slowly.

Fiske was trying to visualize in his mind's eye how a potential battle would play out. It was good to be prepared. He would use every tool at his disposal and fight as dirty as he possibly could in order to beat the Vespers.

They reached the end of the passage. Fiske held up his hand and they all froze.

He took a few more steps forward and peered around the corner.

What he was looking at was a large room with a very high ceiling. So tall was it, in fact, that Fiske could not, in the poor light, actually see the ceiling. He looked all around the room — well, as much of it as he could see. It appeared to be empty. But then again, it could be a trap.

He inched forward some more. He became dimly aware of a large object that was located in a darkened corner of the room at a point farthest away from him.

He looked behind him and observed that the others were following closely.

"Well, I guess it's now or never," said Fiske to himself.

He stepped fully out into the room and prepared to be attacked on all sides.

Nothing happened.

The others formed a ring around him.

"What is that?" Reagan asked, pointing to the far corner.

"I was thinking the same thing," replied Fiske. "I say we find out, shall we?"

They cautiously walked in that direction. As they drew closer the object came into sharper relief.

Its scale was enormous. It must have been fifty feet high and built of metal, wood, and what looked to be sophisticated composites.

To Fiske, it looked like an ancient weapon of mass

destruction that a Roman army might have deployed in battle. But it also looked like a science experiment gone very weird, with long copper tubes weaving in and out of a large, wide, mostly metal body that was rectangular in shape. There were pieces of oddly shaped metal and wood sticking out here and there like appendages that had come as afterthoughts. There were power coils and generator lines and an assortment of objects that Fiske didn't even recognize.

"It looks like something I used to build with my LEGO sets when I was a kid," observed Jonah. "Only a lot bigger, no uniform parts, and with a lot less color."

"Meaning it doesn't look anything *like* a LEGO set," snapped Nellie.

As they stood there, they all suddenly heard the low hum emanating from the device. Fiske put out his hand and touched the core.

"Warm," he noted. "But not exceedingly so. Whatever it is, someone has turned it on. But it doesn't seem at full power yet."

Nellie stared up at the huge creation. "It's creeping me out. It looks like it might come alive at any moment and crush us."

"It does sort of look like that," agreed Fiske. He stepped closer and peered at a spot about midway up the metal core.

"But look there."

They all stared at where he was pointing.

There was a small niche built into the machine. But there was nothing in it.

Jonah looked more closely. "It looks like something is supposed to be inserted in there."

The others looked at him as Jonah's eyes suddenly bulged.

Nellie said, "Jonah, what is it?"

He answered in a quavering voice, "This must be the Doomsday device!" He pointed to the niche. "There was a drawing of Amy's ring in the plans we found in Syracuse. It looked like it would fit right in there."

"The ring?" said Fiske. "What would the ring do?"

"Well, I call it a ring, but I think it was more properly described as a *gear*."

"That's exactly what it is," said a voice.

They all turned to see a young man in a black suit standing within fifteen feet of them. He was holding something.

He said, "One more piece to the puzzle. The final piece, in fact."

Fiske shouted, "Who the bloody hell are you?"

Nellie said, "I recognize the voice. From the room where we met up with Ian."

Fiske looked wildly back at the young man. "This can't be. You? You're . . ."

"Damien Vesper. Not exactly at your service. More precisely, at your demise."

Nellie said in a frightened voice, "Then you're Vesper One?"

"I am indeed," said Damien. "And I hope you hold my image in your mind as your last dying thought."

Fiske looked swiftly around. He could sense others in the darkness, creeping toward them. He took one step back. The others followed his lead.

Buying some time, Fiske said, "So, let me guess. This little thing here is your invention?"

"Mine and Archimedes'," said Damien. "One must give credit where credit is due."

"And what does it do?" asked Fiske.

"I'm Vesper One," said Damien smugly. "Or Damien Vesper, if you prefer. So what do you think it does? Make everyone happy and fulfilled?"

"So mass destruction, then," said Fiske wearily. "Why can't you Vesper types ever think outside the box? It's always plague this, complete annihilation that. It really is very tiresome. Have you ever considered therapy or, at the very least, anger management?"

Damien was unfazed by the sarcasm and didn't respond. But what he did not realize was that Fiske had coiled up the long chain that had been used to immobilize them in the truck and wound it around his waist. Now his hand dipped to the chain and gripped one end of it.

Damien said, "And now I think it's time for you to become hostages once more. But I can promise you that your imprisonment this time will be brief."

"Oh, yeah?" piped in Reagan. "And why is that?"

"Because there is no reason to imprison the dead," replied Damien nastily.

"Touché," said Fiske. "So very predictable of you, Dame."

The figures in the darkness rushed forward at the same time that Fiske uncoiled the chain and, using it like a whip, felled four of the guards who had emerged to try to capture them.

"Go, Cahills!" screamed Fiske. "Fight to the death!!"

All five of them, including the mostly blind Ted Starling and the wounded Nellie, charged ahead to try to do just that.

CHAPTER 30

Dan looked like he might be sick as he knelt next to his sister.

There's so much blood.

He'd also seen how hard Amy had hit the door. He was terrified that she had broken her neck or even her skull. If so, what could they do to help her? They were inside a mountain in the middle of the Rockies and there were probably Vespers lurking all over the place.

"Amy? Ames?" he said quietly, gently applying pressure to her shoulder.

Jake was kneeling on the other side of her while Sinead stood behind him, disbelief on her features.

"Is she . . . is she dead?" asked Sinead. "She . . . she can't be. Not Amy." Sinead started to weep.

"No, I'm not dead," said Amy as she very slowly sat up, rubbing her head.

Dan was so relieved he almost fainted.

Jake hugged her. "Omigosh, Ames, we thought . . ." His voice trailed off as he pulled away and looked at her, tears in his eyes.

She continued to rub her head. "Believe me, I was thinking it, too. That door was hard. Luckily it wasn't as hard as my head."

"But all that blood!" exclaimed Sinead.

"Scalp wound," said Amy matter-of-factly. "They bleed like crazy. But I can already feel it coagulating. I'm good."

"Not so fast," said Dan. "How many fingers am I holding up?" He held up three of them.

"What fingers?" said Amy.

Jake and Dan exchanged terrified glances.

"I'm only kidding, guys," said Amy quickly. "Geez. Get a grip."'

Sinead used some cloths and sterilizing spray from Amy's knapsack to clean up her wound.

As Sinead wound the last bit of gauze around Amy's head, Amy said quietly, "I heard you start to cry when you thought I was dead. There would have been no reason for you to fake that if you thought I was gone."

Sinead didn't answer right away. Finally she looked at Amy, her eyes reddened and swollen. "I've regretted all the awful things I did. I chose the Vespers over the Cahills. That was not only wrong, it was stupid. The choice between good and evil should be an easy one. The fact is, I've always been envious of you, Amy. You're perfect. You have everything. But that was my problem, not yours."

Amy shook her head. "I've always been a little jealous of *you*, Sinead."

"Me? Why?"

"You're so smart and so focused. But of course no one's perfect, are they?"

Sinead zipped the knapsack back up. "I don't expect you to forgive me or trust me. I don't deserve it. I was wicked and I was wrong. But I did what I did because I thought it would be the best chance for my brothers to get better."

Amy looked over at Dan. "I guess if that had happened to Dan it wouldn't have been an easy decision for me, either."

Dan said, "Hey, if you two are finished gabbing, we've got a freaking world to save here."

Sinead rose and held out her hand to Amy. She gripped it and stood.

Amy said, "Are you ready to do this, Sinead?"

Sinead smiled. "I'm ready to go all the way."

Jake started to pull the pistol from his waistband, only it wasn't there.

"Where did it go?" he said frantically.

"I think it got sucked out by the train," said Dan.

"Great, so we've got no weapon."

"We've got our brains. And each other," declared Amy. "I'll take that over a hundred guns."

"You're right, Amy," said Sinead. "We can beat them with our wits. And our teamwork."

"Well, you've got more team to work with now."

They all turned when they heard the voice.

Peering around the corner was Evan.

"Evan!" exclaimed Amy.

He stepped out and was followed by Hamilton, Phoenix, Natalie, and Ian.

Amy ran up to Evan and hugged him.

He looked down at her, his features sort of goofy.

Though she believed she had made her boyfriend decision, the whole Jake-Evan thing had been pushed into the recesses of Amy's mind simply by necessity. She glanced over at Jake and saw him staring at her standing there with her arms around Evan. She quickly let Evan go and stepped back, her cheeks reddening.

He said, "It's so great to see you." He paused. "You've got blood in your hair. And you're all bandaged. Are you okay?"

"She's fine," said Jake, stepping between them. "Right, Ames?"

"I'm fine, Evan," she said. "Thanks for your concern," she added, giving Jake a weird look.

"Wow," said Dan. "Are we super glad to see you dudes."

"Not as glad as we are to see you," said Natalie. "It sucks being a hostage."

"Where are the others?" asked Jake.

"We split up. Five and five," explained Hamilton. "We heard noises and came this way. We thought it might be Vespers, but luckily it was you."

"So the Vespers are here?"

"Cheyenne, Casper, and Sandy are," said Ian. "We

know that for sure. We fought them and ran for it. But there are others."

"Including Isabel," said Amy. "We saw her sneak in here."

"She has Atticus," added Jake miserably. "And if we don't get him back fast, I'm afraid we never will."

"How is Nellie?" asked Dan quickly.

"Wounded, but doing all right," said Hamilton. "She's got a lot of spunk." He suddenly stared at Sinead with unfriendly eyes. "What is she doing here? Isn't she the enemy?" He put a big hand on her shoulder.

"I'm here to find my brother," said Sinead stiffly.

Hamilton said, "Yeah, right. As we understood it, you were Vesper Three, just two notches down from the big guy. You did a lot of bad stuff. I mean a lot." He turned to Amy. "I'm not buying this act. She's lied to us too many times. She's a Vesper through and through."

Sinead ripped Hamilton's hand off her. "I am not a Vesper. I'm an Ekaterina through and through. And my only concern now is finding Ted. And to do that we have to defeat the Vespers."

Hamilton and the other former hostages gazed at her with unfriendly expressions.

Amy stepped in. "Sinead saved our lives back on the train. We wouldn't be here except for her. We have to trust her."

Hamilton shook his head. "Well, excuse me if I don't." He pointed a finger at Sinead. "I'll be watching you."

"Fine," she said. "And I'll be watching *you*." She turned to Evan. "How is Ted?"

"He's okay," said Evan. "He's gotten really good at hearing and sensing things."

"But he's with the others?" said Sinead in a disappointed tone.

"Yeah," said Evan. "But I'm sure they're okay."

Hamilton scoffed, "You're suddenly concerned, Sinead? Didn't you help have him kidnapped?"

"Ever since my brothers were injured, all I've wanted is to help them get back to normal. I worked with whoever would help me do that."

Hamilton looked at Amy. "See, we can't trust her."

Sinead said, "I guess I can understand that. But I want you all to know that Vesper One is going to kill Ted. Therefore, I am not his ally anymore. I'm *your* ally."

Jake cut in. "We can't just stand here yapping. We have to find Att and the others. And we have to stop the Vespers."

"Do you guys hear that?" said Dan suddenly.

They all froze and listened.

Footsteps were coming down the hall. Well, not exactly footsteps. More like people marching.

"We better get going," said Amy. She looked at Hamilton. "Whichever way you guys came from, let's go the other way. Maybe we'll be able to hook up with the others."

"Good idea," said Hamilton. "Come on, Let's go."

They slipped into a corridor and made their way

swiftly down it. The sounds of the marching faded away.

Amy said, "We think we know why Isabel is here."

"Why?" asked Evan.

"There's a massive subduction zone right under our feet. The Doomsday device must be located here. Somewhere."

Natalie said, "But if my mother had to go to the museum to figure that out . . . ?"

Amy said, "Exactly. She wasn't in on the plan. She's Vesper Two, but wants to be Vesper One, obviously. And Vesper One is just as obviously having nothing to do with that. They clearly don't trust each other."

"Smart of both of them," added Sinead dryly.

Dan said, "The point is, Isabel is here to try to take over. I just know it."

Sinead said, "With Isabel and Vesper One going at each other, it might give us an opportunity."

Amy said, "We have to find the others. Come on."

She hurried down the hall and everyone followed.

CHAPTER 31

Sandy awoke first and rubbed his head. He slowly got to his feet and eyed Cheyenne and then Casper. They were both still lying on the floor, unconscious. But as he watched, he saw them start to stir.

Casper sat up, groaning and massaging the back of his neck. Then Cheyenne came to and put her head between her knees. She looked like she might be sick.

"Well, that was simply brilliant," snapped Sandy as he hovered over them.

Casper looked up and snarled, "Shut up. I didn't exactly see you fighting."

"I saw you running away, in fact," added Cheyenne. "Vesper One will not like that when we tell him."

"My goodness, you two are so out of things it's extraordinary, it really is. You're going to go to Vesper One and complain that I didn't fight well enough even though you two, who were brought on for your sup-posed *muscle*, were defeated by a bunch of kids and one old man!"

"Hamilton is *not* a little kid," barked Casper. "The dude can hit."

"And Fiske Cahill is a master at martial arts," said Cheyenne. "He's not some punk like you."

"Well, regardless, it's now time to pay the piper, as they say."

Casper and Cheyenne stood and faced Sandy.

She said, "And what exactly does that mean?"

"It means exactly THIS."

Sandy's hand shot out of his pocket. In it was a spray can. He hit the button and a concentrated stream of air hit Cheyenne in the face.

"Hey!" yelled Casper. He lunged forward as his sister fell to the floor.

The spray next hit Casper in the face. A second later he lay paralyzed next to Cheyenne.

Sandy stood over them and smiled triumphantly.

"Such silliness. Did you really think you could have beaten us?" He put his hands on his hips. "And they say weathermen aren't tough. HA!"

His phone buzzed. He answered it.

"Yes, I understand. It will be done. Disloyalty cannot be tolerated."

He put the phone away, grabbed Cheyenne's arms, and started to slide her from the room.

"Away we go to your doom," said Sandy. "I'm really starting to enjoy myself."

Isabel stopped walking, turned, and looked behind her. Her men stared resolutely back at her. They were good men, loyal to her, but there weren't that many of them. Vesper One would have far more assets than she.

She stared down at Atticus, who was looking up at her with hatred.

She kicked him. "Stop looking at me like that, you little nothing."

"I'm not a nothing. I'm the last Guardian!"

She laughed and kicked him again for good measure. "Yes, the great and good Guardian. My prisoner. Soon to be dead. How powerful you are."

"I would advise you to give yourself up. It's your only chance."

She laughed again. "Well, you have courage, I'll give you that. But it is far outweighed by your complete and utter stupidity!"

Isabel looked in front of her, trying to figure out where to go next.

"So where's the Doomsday device?" asked Atticus, peering up at her again.

She shot him a furious glance. "What do you know about that?"

"Pretty much everything."

"You can't possibly."

"Now who's being completely and utterly stupid?" She kicked him again, harder.

He straightened back up, shrugging off the effects

of her latest blow. "You're getting soft. Barely felt that one."

She grabbed him by the collar and slammed him up against the rock wall.

"What do you know about it?"

He looked at her, understanding settling over his features. "Wow, he didn't tell you? Amazing. Vesper One must have a problem with his second-in-command."

"Shut up! Now, tell me."

"What do you want me to do? Shut up or tell you?" he said imperturbably. "I can't do *both*."

She shook him, lifting his heels off the floor with her rage.

"Do not be impertinent. Talk. Now!"

"Well, it's Archimedes', isn't it? One of his inventions. It uses the corollary strength of nearby subduction zones to create a massive power surge. It's already been initiated."

"And you know that how?" scoffed Isabel.

"Uh, duh. Why do you think you had to take a train here as opposed to a plane?"

"So *that* was the reason? I suspected, of course. Something is going on."

"Well, we more than suspected, we knew. It's messing with the magnetic polarity of the Earth."

She stared at him curiously. "And that's bad?"

"Are you kidding?"

She snapped, "I am first-rate with poisons. A genius, in fact. I'm an amazing code breaker. I didn't have the code to get into this place, but solved it. I have drunk the Lucian serum. The only one in the world to have done so. I'm in my late forties but look like I'm thirty-three. And on my good days and depending on the light I can pass for midtwenties. But I am not, and never have been, brilliant in the physical sciences." She shook him again.

Atticus said, "Uh, TMI, but that's okay. To answer your questions, reversing the polarity of the Earth's poles I would put squarely in the category of utterly and irreversibly catastrophic, not simply bad." He stared at her. "You gave a speech at the train station about AWW."

"I believe in it," Isabel declared.

"Uh, yeah. That goes in the 'what the crap, you think I'm that stupid?' category. But listen, even if you want to capitalize on the catastrophic damage to look like some savior, it won't matter."

She looked at him darkly. "Why not?"

"Hello? I've already told you. When you mess with the polarity of the Earth then there will be no more Earth. If there's no Earth I'm not sure how you can be the savior of it. Just employing standard logical reasoning, you understand."

"You're a fool."

"Okay, and so what does that make Vesper One? He wants to destroy the world. Where is he going to live? Where are *you* going to live? Got a moon colony we don't know about?"

Atticus didn't really know what Vesper One's plan was. But he had an incentive right this instant to make the "Doomsday" argument sound very real.

Isabel smirked. "He is not going to destroy the entire world, you idiot."

"Okay, which part gets to survive? This piece of terra firma will be no more when he cranks the sucker up."

Isabel glanced at her men. They were eyeing one another nervously. She looked back at Atticus. "So you're saying that he plans to destroy the part of the Earth where we are right now? But *he's* here! I know he is. How does that make sense? He'll die, too."

"Oh, I don't know, maybe he's suicidal. Ever think of that possibility?"

Isabel hissed like a snake and glanced at her men once more. They were all taking steps back.

"What are you doing?" she snapped. "Don't listen to him. He's only a child."

The men turned and ran flat out.

"Come back! Come back!"

Before she could make another move, her men were out of sight.

She looked down at Atticus and shook him hard. "You fool. You did that on purpose. And now you've cost me my henchmen."

"I just wanted you to be fully informed as to the conditions on the ground. So, are you going to stick around for the big boom?"

"Idiot boy. I—"

Atticus shrieked and pointed. "Vesper One! There!"

Isabel didn't look that way. "Do you really think I'm that stupid?"

Atticus slipped one hand inside his pocket. A second later the sounds of an MP5 machine gun blasted through the tunnels.

Isabel ducked, rolled, and pulled a large gun from her coat pocket.

When she got back to her feet, Atticus was gone.

She had no idea that Dan had told Atticus exactly how he had fooled Isabel and her henchmen back in DC. Or that Atticus had loaded that same sound track on his phone and engaged it by pushing a button when he'd slipped his hand in his pocket. That tactic had just paid huge dividends.

She heard his footsteps running away, but with all the tunnels here, it was impossible to determine in which direction he'd gone. But she didn't need him, anyway. However, what he had told Isabel had been valuable. To think that the idiot Vesper One would even contemplate such a thing. But it couldn't be true, could it? It was one thing to beat the Cahills and rule the world. It was a very different thing to destroy the world entirely.

I live here, too.

She looked down at the knapsack she'd been carrying. It belonged to that simpering Dan Cahill. She smiled. If she had figured correctly, it was more than worth its weight in gold. All her little texts under the name of Arthur Josiah Trent to his adoring, gullible son were about to pay off.

She opened the knapsack and dug through it.

It took her a minute, but she found it.

She held up the silver flask.

The serum.

Finally. She had it.

And with it she perhaps had a way to win after all.

CHAPTER 32

"Oooff," Jake exclaimed as he turned a corner and ran hard into something. The "something" fell backward and Jake landed on top of it.

"Atticus!"

Jake quickly lifted his little brother up and dusted him off as the others gathered around.

Jake hugged Atticus so hard his brother gasped in pain.

"Att, I wasn't sure I'd ever see you alive again."

"Well, if you keep squeezing him that hard, he might not stay alive," pointed out Sinead.

Jake let him go and stepped back, a broad grin on his face.

"How did you get away, Att?" asked Dan.

"Just a little misdirection," he said, obviously pleased with himself. Just then, Atticus seemed to notice the others. He flashed a huge smile. "You guys got away, too!"

Evan nodded. "We split up. Fiske took four others

and headed out in another direction. I hope they're okay."

Atticus smacked knuckles with Phoenix and smiled shyly at Natalie, who had regained a little of her haughtiness and didn't smile at him.

"So, what do we do now?" asked Jake.

Amy looked around. "Preferably hook up with the others, locate the Doomsday device, and somehow disable it."

"That's a lot to ask for," said Hamilton.

"Go big or go home," declared Dan.

Atticus looked at him. "Isabel has your knapsack."

Dan's features clouded. Amy gazed at him worriedly. Hamilton caught this look.

"Something we need to know? What's in Dan's knapsack?"

Amy stared at Dan but said nothing.

Dan sighed. "The serum."

"What!" exclaimed the former hostages in unison.

Jake looked accusingly at Amy. "You didn't tell me that."

Ian said, "So, our mother finally has the serum. She'll take it. And when she does, there will be no stopping her."

"Maybe," said Amy. "But maybe we won't want to stop her."

They all stared at her.

"How exactly does that make sense?" asked Evan.

"Oh, it makes a lot of sense from a historical perspective," replied Amy. "But we don't have time to sit here and debate this. We have to find the others. And we have to do it fast."

Jake said, "She's right. Come on."

They ran hard down several corridors, turning left at some and right at others.

Every once in a while Amy would look down at her phone-app compass. It had worked pretty well before, despite their being inside a mountain. But now it was jumping all over the place.

Something was coming. She wondered if it could be stopped. Maybe it was already too late.

They reached a broad passageway, far wider than any of the others they had encountered. Amy stopped and said, "Let's take a minute and get our bearings."

"Look," exclaimed Dan.

They all stared at where he was pointing.

Jake said, "It's a door. First one we've seen."

"It's a *big* door," added Atticus, staring up at the ten-foot-high wooden portal.

Sinead stepped forward. "Well, instead of standing here gawking at it, perhaps we should see if it's open. How's that for an idea?"

"Now that's the Sinead we all know and loathe," said Dan.

When she whipped around to stare piercingly at him, he smiled and said, "That nicey-nice junk just wasn't you, Sinead. Be yourself."

She started to snap something back but then

apparently reconsidered. She actually smiled at him. "Good advice."

Hamilton added, "By that, I hope you don't mean you're going back to your evil, deceitful ways."

"No, I'm just not going to keep on trying to prove by words that I'm on your side. I'll let my *actions* do it."

She yanked hard on the door's immense wrought-iron handle and, to everyone's surprise, it opened easily.

They cautiously peered inside the chamber. It was large and totally dark.

"Should we go in?" asked Natalie in a quavering voice.

"I guess we better," Amy whispered back. "The others might be in here, only we might not be able to see them."

"Or they could be hurt, or worse," added Evan.

They all eased into the room.

When Hamilton, the last one in because he was guarding their rear flank, stepped clear of the door, it slammed shut and locked.

They all whirled around to look at it.

Amy said accusingly, "Ham, why did you shut the door?"

"I didn't. It closed all by itself."

"Never a good thing," opined Atticus nervously. "Doors closing by themselves."

Suddenly, the lights came on in a blinding flash, causing all of them to shield their eyes with their hands.

"Wow," said Ian painfully. "Where did that come from?"

"Uh, guys?" said Atticus, who was looking upward.

Dan tugged on the door. "It won't open."

"Let me try," said Hamilton.

"Uh, guys!" said Atticus more urgently.

Hamilton tugged on the door with all his strength. Nothing happened.

"Let me help," said Jake. He and Hamilton pulled hard on the handle.

"Guys!" snapped Atticus.

"What is it, Att?" barked his brother. "We're busy over here."

Atticus pointed upward. "Look!"

Everyone slowly looked in that direction.

Suspended in the air, their hands tied above them with chains, were Cheyenne and Casper. They appeared to be unconscious.

"What the—" began Dan.

Atticus blurted, "Does anyone else hear that?"

That was the sound of something gurgling.

"What's that?" exclaimed Natalie as something touched her foot and she jumped.

Now instead of looking up they all looked down.

It was water. Lots of it. And it was coming fast from somewhere.

"The room is filling up," shouted Jake.

Indeed it was. The water level was already at their calves.

Amy yelled, "Quick, the door, we have to get it open!"

They ran over to the door and everyone pulled and tugged and kicked and pushed. The heavy wood didn't budge.

"We're trapped!" yelled Dan.

"We're going to die!" added a frantic Natalie.

The water was now up to their waists and it was rising fast.

There seemed to be no way out.

Dan and Amy looked at each other.

Dan was thinking, *If I had the serum, I could take it and break the door down. But I don't and I can't.*

Amy seemed to be reading his thoughts. She inexplicably smiled at him. It was a calming smile.

It seemed to say that they would get out of this, somehow.

But as the water inched up toward their chests and Jake put Atticus on his shoulders to keep him above the waterline, Dan couldn't see any way out of this one. As the torrent kept pouring in, they all started to tread water.

Phoenix was struggling, and Hamilton quickly went to his aid, keeping his head above the water.

Amy looked at the others as they slowly floated up to the ceiling.

This is it. We're going to die.

CHAPTER 33

Fiske Cahill was fighting like a man thirty years younger. He had destroyed three of Vesper One's men but others kept coming. As he looked around he saw that his group was slowly losing the battle.

Nellie had struggled valiantly with one Vesper, but he had pounded her on her injured shoulder and she was now facedown on the floor with her hands zip-cuffed behind her.

Reagan was fighting like a demon, leveling every Vesper that came within her reach. But Fiske watched helplessly as another Vesper Tasered the teenage tornado and she instantly dropped to the floor and out of the fight.

Jonah had been subdued almost immediately, although he kept trash-talking after his hands were bound behind him until one of the Vespers stuffed a rag in his mouth.

Jonah's last words before this happened were "You wanna 'nother piece of me, bro?"

And poor Ted was swinging randomly at Vespers

who surrounded him. They laughed at his awkward attempts to hit them until one drew too close and Ted connected and knocked him flat on his butt. Then they quickly subdued him.

Fiske fought on, the last man standing. But as a dozen Vespers formed a circle around him he knew it was only a matter of time. He looked behind him at the behemoth device.

If he could somehow sabotage it . . . ?

He turned, ran straight at a slight gap in the Vespers' defensive arc, broke through by flattening two Vespers with one spin kick, and sprinted flat out at the device.

A single shot rang out.

Fiske Cahill gasped and fell to the floor.

Amy looked frantically around. Their heads were maybe a foot from the ceiling. She looked at the Wyoming twins. Because of how they were strung up, their mouths were very nearly underwater. As Cheyenne drew some water into her lungs, she suddenly jerked and awakened. Amy watched as the tall young woman darted glances around the room and saw her brother trussed up beside her. Then her gaze fell on Amy and the others.

Amy shouted, "We found you tied up here. Then the water started pouring in. We're going to die!"

Cheyenne struggled against her bindings, but to no avail. She started to swing herself sideways. It was hard, being mostly in the water, but she kept at it. She finally managed to hit her brother but then bounced off. The second time she collided with him, Casper woke up, too.

Cheyenne screamed, "Sandy did this. He's working with Vesper One. We're going to die."

Casper looked frantically around and saw Amy floating near him. Amy wasn't looking at him. She was staring at the door. The walls were solid stone. The water was having no effect on them. But the door was wood and, thick though it was, it was not nearly as strong as the walls. And water could always escape through a weaker part of whatever was trying to contain it.

But she needed something to work with.

She turned back to the Wyomings.

"Do you have something that I can try to open the door with?"

Cheyenne looked at her brother.

"Knife, in a sheath on his left leg."

Amy took a breath, held it, and dove under the water.

It was cold and dark but she made her way over to Casper, felt for his leg, slipped up his pant leg, gripped the knife, and pulled it free from its sheath.

She surfaced.

Dan looked at her. "What are you doing?"

"Trying to save us," she called back. She dove back under and kicked hard to make herself go deeper. She reached the door and thrust the knife in between the door and the door frame at the point where the lock would be located. She pulled back on the knife handle, trying to jerk back the lock with it. Her air almost out, she kicked to the surface.

She looked around. Casper and Cheyenne were now underwater.

"Jake, Evan!"

They looked at her and she pointed frantically at the Wyomings.

Atticus said, "It's okay, Jake. I can tread water."

"Not for much longer," grumbled Jake. They were almost at the ceiling.

Evan and Jake swam over to the Wyomings and managed to lift their heads out of the water by holding on to the chains and using them as leverage.

Cheyenne and Casper both gasped for air when their heads broke the water's surface.

Amy dove back down and began working on the lock again. Twice she managed to wedge the knife into the correct position, and both times she didn't have the strength to pull it back.

If she went back up to draw in air, she was afraid there would be no "up" to get it. The entire room would be underwater.

This would be her last chance. She dug the knife in and pulled with all her strength, even planting her feet against the solid wall to increase her leverage. It didn't work.

Then Amy felt something tugging on the knife. She looked over and Dan was next to her, helping her. Together they pulled with all their might.

Amy could feel the lock slowly sliding back.

WHOOSH!

It was like a mini-tsunami. The door, pushed by tons of water, shot open and the freed water poured through it.

And so did all of them.

They were hurled pell-mell down the hall. As the water dissipated, they all groaned and slowly got to their feet, checking for broken bones and missing limbs.

Amy looked at Dan, who was next to her.

"Thanks," she said. "I couldn't have done it alone."

"What little brothers are for. That and making big sisters crazy," he said, though the terror of almost drowning was still clearly in his features.

Jake pointed back toward the room where the Wyomings were still dangling.

"What about them?"

"Leave them," said Amy. "Gives us two fewer jerks we have to fight. I think we'll have enough to face as it is. Let's go."

They all ran off to finish this.

CHAPTER 34

Fiske lay motionless for a long moment. The pain in his shoulder burned like someone had pierced him with a sword covered with molten lava. That's what it felt like to be shot. He rolled over and rose to his knees, feeling slightly nauseous.

He looked up to see everyone staring at him. Nellie gazed grimly at him and touched her own gunshot wound. Reagan, the effects of the Taser wearing off, stared at him with semi-paralyzed features. Ted could not see him, but apparently could sense what had happened.

"Fiske?" he said. "Are you okay?"

Jonah just grunted with the rag stuffed in his mouth.

Fiske managed to say, "I'm all right." However, he felt far from all right.

"For now," said Vesper One as he walked into the circle formed by his men. "But not for long," he added, the smoking gun still in his hand.

Fiske stared up at him.

"You know, for an evil genius type with delusions of grandeur, I really would have pegged you for being a bit longer in the tooth. You look like you're about to go to the prom for the first time, not that any decent girl would condescend to go with a creepy punk like you."

Vesper One's expression remained unchanged. "Sarcasm flowing from a defeated foe. Interesting. I guess if it makes you feel better, go right ahead."

"You don't want me to really get started. I might never stop."

Vesper One gazed at him with pity. "Oh, you'll stop. Precisely when I want you to." He pointed the muzzle of his pistol at the center of Fiske's broad forehead.

"Shoot an unarmed man? Hardly sporting of you."

"But I'm not sporting. I'm a Vesper. I win any way I can."

"Actually, so do the Cahills."

This comment had not come from Fiske.

It had come from Amy Cahill.

The next instant Vesper One's minions were being overwhelmed by this infusion of fresh troops.

Jake brought down two of them all by himself, pounding them until they collapsed into unconsciousness.

Hamilton moved through the Vespers like a threshing machine, kicking and punching any of them within reach. When one tried to Taser him, he grabbed the device and zapped the man instead.

Amy and Dan stood back-to-back and took on all

comers. Kicking and punching and biting when necessary, they managed to subdue a half dozen Vespers in a matter of minutes.

Evan had one Vesper in a headlock when the shot rang out. At first Evan didn't seem to have noticed that he'd been hit. Then he looked down at his chest and saw the blood flowing from the hole there. He fell to the floor. The others were so busy fighting they didn't notice.

Ian and Natalie were kicking and punching as they worked their way to the Doomsday device. Natalie finally broke through a column of Vespers and ran for it, after picking up a large metal bar one of the Vespers had dropped. She swung it back, ready to deliver a crushing blow to the huge machine.

Ian watched in admiration until he noticed the blue sparks spewing from the base of the device.

"Natalie, no!"

She didn't hear him.

She swung the pole and hit her target squarely in the middle. It did no damage. To the device. Natalie stood there, momentarily frozen as the electrical current built up in the device swept through her.

Ian watched, paralyzed by panic as his sister was hit by the current. He didn't know what to do. He couldn't exactly fathom what was happening.

Then the surge of power from the Doomsday device ceased, and the metal bar fell away. Natalie moaned once and fell to the floor.

"No!" screamed Ian as he fought his way to his sister.

He knelt next to her. Her eyes were open. He felt for a pulse. There was none.

He started performing CPR. He pumped and pumped her chest, trying to restart her heart. He kept checking her pulse. Finally, he sat back, exhausted. He stared down at his sister. The truth was something that Ian could not comprehend, though it was crystal clear.

Natalie Kabra was dead.

As the fighting continued all around him, Ian sat there on his haunches overcome with anguish. He had just been reunited with his sister and now he had lost her. He couldn't quite understand that she would not be coming back. How could she be dead? She was always so much alive. In everything she did. Ian had so looked forward to growing up with her. They were all each other had. All the family left of the Kabras.

He reached down and touched her cheek. It was still warm. He touched her hand. It felt so limp, but instead of pulling away, Ian gripped it more tightly, as though his warmth could bring her back. But of course it couldn't. The dead could not come back.

The laughter reached Ian's ears a moment later. He looked over and saw Vesper One in the far corner. He held up a device that looked like a remote.

"A *shocking* experience for her, wouldn't you say, Ian?" crowed Vesper One.

Enraged, Ian slowly rose, smashed his way through

two Vespers, and charged straight at Vesper One.

"You die, right now," yelled Ian. He had never truly imagined killing anyone until right this instant. Now he could not exist another second while this man lived.

"So many have said, and yet here I am," taunted Vesper One.

In another moment he was gone.

Ian couldn't believe his eyes. He looked around everywhere.

How had he disappeared?

Amy came running over to him. "I'm so sorry, Ian." The tears in her eyes matched the ones in his. She had obviously seen Natalie's body.

Ian panted. "I will get him. If it's the last thing I do. I will get him."

"*We'll* get him, Ian. All of us."

"All of us who are *left*," he amended bitterly, staring over at his dead sister.

They turned back to the fight.

That's when Amy saw him.

Evan, on the floor, blood flowing out of his chest.

"NO!" screamed Amy. She ran toward Evan, flooring a Vesper with a kick to the head as she zipped past.

She reached Evan and knelt down next to him. His eyes were closed. She felt for a pulse. It was there, but just a trickle.

"Evan, can you hear me?"

He opened his eyes, managed a smile. "Boy, this sucks, right?"

He laughed feebly.

All Amy could do was let the tears slide down her face. She took off her sweater, balled it up, and placed it over his wound.

"You're going to be fine, Evan. I swear."

"Amy, look out!" screamed Dan.

Amy ducked and the sword missed her by an inch. The Vesper holding it reared back to try again. But he had picked the wrong time to try to kill her.

Amy lashed out with a tremendous kick and the man toppled to the floor.

As she turned back to Evan, she heard a little gasp.

She looked down at him. His eyes were open. But they were no longer seeing. His arms slid off his chest and lay limp next to him.

Amy took one long, shuddering breath, and then closed Evan's eyes.

Then she rose, turned, and plunged back into the fight. But there was only one person she wanted to destroy.

Vesper One.

And she would. Or die trying.

Whatever happened, one of them would not see the sun rise ever again.

CHAPTER 35

They beat back the Vespers, forcing them from the room where the Doomsday device was located. Hamilton and Jake had managed to wrench several guns from the Vespers. They each had one and had given one to Amy and the last weapon to Reagan.

They had carried the bodies of Natalie and Evan to a far corner and found blankets to cover them. Amy and Sinead were cleaning and bandaging Fiske Cahill's injured shoulder. Fortunately, the bullet had gone clean through. But he was in a lot of pain, though he tried not to show it. As they were working on him he kept staring over at the two bodies under the blankets.

"That should be me under there," he told Amy and Sinead. "Not Evan and Natalie. I'm old. They had their whole lives ahead of them."

Amy said nothing. She just kept winding gauze around Fiske's shoulder and arm.

Sinead said, "Before this is over, we might all be dead."

"Cheery thought," said Dan as he joined them.

They had posted sentries at all entry points to the room. Hamilton, Reagan, and Jake, being the most athletic and having guns, had taken the first watch and intently gazed at all possible attack points.

There were thirteen of them left now, thought Amy. Maybe an unlucky thirteen.

"You're good to go," said Amy as she applied the last bit of adhesive to Fiske's dressings.

"Thank you, Amy." He looked over at the bodies. "Alistair, now Natalie and Evan."

"It would have been ridiculous to think that everyone could survive this," said Sinead logically, if dispassionately.

Amy wasn't listening to her. She stared up at the Doomsday device. Ian had already told them about the electrical charge, so they knew not to touch it. She wondered what was going on outside this mountain. Had catastrophe already struck? What would happen if it were fully initiated?

She turned to Sinead, Dan, and Atticus, who had come to sit next to them. "Talk to me about subduction zones. I've read about them, but I need to know more."

"What do you want to know?" asked Atticus.

"If I have it right, we're sitting on a big one."

Sinead said, "Yes, as I explained on the train before. It stretches a long way both east and west."

"So if the device taps into it, the destruction would follow that exact route, *both* ways?" asked Amy.

Atticus looked unsure. So did Sinead.

Dan said, "I guess I see what you're getting at. Vesper One brought the hostages here. He's here. If he starts this sucker up, then both the hostages and he would be the first to die."

"That's what had Isabel confused, too," added Atticus. "I guess she thought Vesper One was far too vain to take his own life."

"Reversing the polarity of the magnetic poles," said Amy. "Results?"

Fiske rubbed his injured shoulder and sat back against the rock wall. "So, that's what we're talking about here? Reversing magnetic polarity?"

"Well, it's about subduction zones, too," amended Amy.

"All right. I can give you a little insight into both, actually."

"You can?" said Amy.

"I've traveled all over the world, particularly in my youth. Spent some time at a research facility in Amsterdam that specialized in collecting data on the Earth's magnetic poles. When I was in Japan I learned about subduction zones from a scientist there studying tsunamis."

"Cool," said Dan. "We know if you reverse the poles it's catastrophic."

Fiske looked at him curiously. "Actually, the magnetic poles of the Earth have reversed many times over the eons."

"What?" exclaimed Dan and Atticus together.

"Oh, yes. The last time was nearly eight hundred thousand years ago, so I don't exactly recall the details. Even I'm not *that* old. And on a daily basis, the magnetic poles can wander up to fifty miles."

Amy looked confused. "But how is that possible? Our research showed it could be catastrophic, cause all sorts of natural disasters."

Fiske explained, "The Earth's magnetic field protects us from cosmic radiation. The field itself is produced by interaction of the Earth's solid inner iron core with its outer liquid one. When the poles reverse, the field never actually dips to zero. But even if it did, we would be protected by the sun's magnetic field, which, by the way, reverses polarity every nine to twelve years."

Dan said, "So am I getting this right? Reversing the polarity of the Earth is *not* a big deal? Because apparently old Archimedes thought it was and he was, like, freaking brilliant."

Fiske rubbed his shoulder and grimaced. "I didn't say that, Danny boy. Ordinarily, reversing the polarity takes place over thousands of years. People and other living things have time to adapt, and so does the Earth and its axial rotational spectrum."

Amy nodded in understanding. "But if it happened really quickly? Not over several thousand years, but maybe in a matter of minutes? I think that's what Archimedes was afraid of."

"A trial run for the Vespers," said Dan bitterly.

Fiske nodded slowly. "Given that, all bets are off.

Now, when you couple accelerated reverse polarity with proximity to a major subduction zone, it's like a match and a river of fuel. The accelerated reverse polarity is the match and the subduction zone, is the river of fuel. The catastrophic results would stretch far and wide. Natural disaster piled on natural disaster. Not pretty."

They all looked up at the Doomsday device.

"And that may be the key to it all," said Amy.

Ian came over and pointed to the empty niche in the center of the device. "So long as we keep the last component out of there, we can stop it. That's the place for the gear to be inserted. I'm sure of it."

"I think you're right, Ian," said Amy.

"But how long can we do that?" said Dan. "And we can't destroy the thing. We can't even touch it without being electrocuted."

Fiske nodded. "And at some point Vesper One will regroup his people and attack. And if we can't beat them off, he'll be able to execute his plan."

They all sat there looking glum.

Dan said, "So we just sit here waiting for them to come? That seems stupid."

Amy looked up at the Doomsday device. For her it represented the culmination, perversely, of their traveling the globe involuntarily to do Vesper One's bidding.

She looked over at Dan, who was staring up at the monstrosity, too. He glanced at her.

"We made this possible," he said starkly.

"What choice did we have?" she asked.

"We sacrificed the world for a few friends and family," said Dan, just as starkly.

"We didn't know that at the time," she pointed out in a sharp tone.

"We could have guessed. Vesper One was not exactly doing all this for the good of mankind. We had to know that it would turn out bad."

Amy looked over at the bodies of Natalie and Evan. Dan followed her gaze. They exchanged a silent look.

"Maybe you're right," said Amy. "And maybe I screwed up big-time. Some leader I turned out to be."

"It's not over yet, Amy," said Fiske, studying her quietly. "And let's look at the positives."

"Like what?" she asked grimly.

"Well, let's see. You figured out what the plan was. You got in this place. You helped rescue us. We are now in a position to stop Vesper One."

"And Natalie and Evan are dead. So is Alistair."

"And we could all die, too," said Fiske. "But you have put us in a position where we have a chance. A shot to make this right. To make sure that Alistair and Evan and Natalie didn't die in vain."

Amy thought about this for a few moments and finally nodded. "You're right, Fiske. You're a good uncle."

"I wouldn't go that far. But I have my moments."

"So, what do we do?" asked Dan in exasperation. "To stop them?"

CHAPTER 36

Amy gazed up at the device. A sudden shift in the poles, as Fiske had pointed out, would be catastrophic. But how did they stop it from happening? At that instant something occurred to her.

She looked at Fiske and Dan, who were nearby. "I don't think Vesper One is the suicidal type."

"What do you mean?" asked Fiske.

"He wants to rule the world, not leave it. And Sinead showed me the subduction zones on the computer while we were on the train. She said they worked like underground rivers, or maybe oceans. They create a tsunami, building pressure, which then races off to do damage at some other place. The zone under us runs both east and west, but I don't think they're connected. So if the device creates a tsunami effect here . . . ?"

Dan said, "Then it'll build, but do no damage, at its origins."

Fiske added, "But it'll build over time, and when it hits its target—"

Amy finished for him, "It'll be obliterated."

"Wow, that's a relief," said Dan sarcastically. "So at least we won't die in a tsunami. We'll just be murdered by the Vespers."

Amy ignored him and looked over in a corner, where there were some wooden crates piled high. She opened a few. Inside were just some copper wires and other odds and ends that Vesper One must have used to construct the device. She closed the last crate.

"There must be a series of electromagnets built in there," she said, pointing at the device. "Powerful ones."

"I would imagine there are," agreed Fiske.

Amy continued, "But there are different ways to create electric and magnetic fields. A changing electrical field creates a magnetic field and vice versa. That's what makes generators and motors possible. A weakening electrical signal creates a stronger magnetic field, and then the reverse is also true."

"So exactly how does that help us?" asked Dan in exasperation. "I feel like I'm in a physics class. And I'm not even in high school."

"Magnetic fields created by electrical currents cease to be when the electrical current stops," replied Amy.

"That's right," said Fiske. "No power, no electromagnetic field."

"Hello?" said Dan. "That sucker has plenty of power. It's electrified."

"But I wonder what its source is," mulled Amy, looking around the base. "There has to be a source of electrical power. If we can somehow find it and turn it off . . . ?"

"Then the device will be rendered inoperable," said Fiske.

Atticus said, "But how do we turn it off?"

Amy, Dan, and Fiske stared helplessly at one another.

"Maybe if we had some water we could create a short circuit," said Fiske.

"We had a lot of water in another room," replied Dan. "But I don't see a faucet in here."

Amy said, "We could try throwing things at it."

She picked up the metal bar that Natalie had used. "Stand back," she said. She threw the bar at the device. It struck against it, held there for a moment, and then fell away.

"Well, that didn't work," pointed out Dan unnecessarily.

Fiske said quietly, "I think, Amy, that the only option we have is to keep the Vespers from reaching the device."

"Meaning this is our Waterloo," said Dan. "Our Custer's Last Stand," he added grimly.

Fiske nodded. "I think it might be, because I don't see any other way out."

"Well, if that's the way it's going to be, so be it," said Amy resignedly.

She watched as Sinead joined her brother, who was sitting with his back to a wall. As Amy continued to look on, Sinead put her arms around Ted and quietly spoke to him. Amy looked over at Dan and saw him watching the Starlings as well.

Dan and Amy exchanged an understanding glance.

Dan moved next to Amy and said, "I guess, being triplets, the Starlings have a really close bond."

"I don't think that's limited to triplets, Dan. I think it goes for all brothers and sisters. Or it should, anyway."

"Do you think the serum might actually help Ted and Ned?" Dan asked.

"It's not worth it, Dan. It never was. The effects are so unknown, it could easily end up doing far more harm than good. I think Sinead realized that, too. She knows that Vesper One only used her because he knew she wanted to help her brothers so badly." She broke off and looked at Sinead again. "And maybe there's something a lot stronger and purer anyway that will help them get better."

"What's that?" asked Dan.

"Love. The most powerful thing in the universe."

As she said it Amy glanced once more over at Evan's body. Her eyes began to tear up.

Dan noticed this and put an arm around her, leading her off to the side and helping her to sit down as her body shook. The shaking gave way to shudders and sobbing and then gasping. And then Amy Cahill dried her eyes and sat up straight.

"Fiske was right."

"About what?"

"If we don't finish this, if we don't beat the Vespers, everyone will have died in vain."

"Well, we are going to beat them," said Dan. "Guaranteed. Done deal!"

Amy gazed proudly at him. "I can always count on you to lift my spirits."

"When I'm not bugging the crap out of you."

"And don't I know it."

Dan looked over at Natalie's body. Ian sat next to it, his head on his drawn-up knees, his eyes closed, the tears sliding down his cheeks.

Dan asked, "Do you think Isabel will even care . . . about Natalie?"

Amy wiped her eyes one last time. "I would like to think that every mother would care about losing her child. That no matter how evil and ruthless you are, you would care about your own flesh and blood." She paused. "But with Isabel I'm not sure. She's not like other mothers. She's not like other human beings, for that matter."

"That's okay. We'll care."

She tousled his hair.

"Yes, we will."

CHAPTER 37

"We're running out of time."

Sandy was pacing back and forth in front of Vesper One. They were cloistered in Vesper One's command center, which had TV screens showing all activity going on in the tunnels by way of hidden surveillance cameras embedded in the walls.

Vesper One was not looking at him. He was watching the screen showing the room where Amy and the others were. And his precious Doomsday device.

"I don't like that they're in there and we're not," whined Vesper One.

"Yes, it is not an ideal situation," replied Sandy, keeping his voice purposely even and calm. He had dealt with Vesper One many times and, though brilliant, he was still very young and prone to irrational actions, as were many young people with limited experience in the world. Sandy had been around the block more than a few times. He knew never to lose sight of the end game.

"They're in there with *my* machine," said a petulant Vesper One.

"Yes, but it's electrified and they can't touch it, much less disable it. But as I said, we're running out of time." Sandy checked a display on a computer screen that he had programmed to monitor all meteorological data in the world.

He eyed the flow of data and said in a warning tone, "By my calculations our window of opportunity will be incredibly narrow. Perhaps no more than five minutes."

Vesper One focused on him for the first time. His features held the annoyed look of a child who had been denied his favorite toy.

"And the result? You're sure?"

"The subduction zone interactive magnification multiplier formulas are very straightforward and surprisingly easy to calculate with enviable accuracy. If only predicting the weather were as reliable."

"And the result?" persisted Vesper One.

"The city of Chicago and its three million–plus inhabitants will be under a hundred feet of water after Lake Michigan escapes its banks and floods the entire area. The loss of life will be catastrophic, the damage to property incalculable. The third-largest city in the country will be completely destroyed."

"Impressive," said Vesper One.

Sandy's eyes shone. "And I will be there, after it's over, of course, and a suitable level of safety has been ensured, to cover it all. I will be known the world over as the meteorologist who cares in the aftermath of disaster. A disaster I helped cause, of course, but that's simply a technicality. Ah, the blissful ignorance of the public; it's truly a wonderful thing."

"Exactly how much time do we have?" asked Vesper One. He obviously did not care about Sandy's aspirations to be a world-beloved weatherman.

"One hour — no more, no less," Sandy said matter-of-factly after gazing at his meteorological data. "Oh, and a few more things you need to know."

Vesper One glared at him. Sandy's tone had been a bit too condescending.

Sandy, realizing this, quickly changed tactics. "As the leader of the Vespers, you must have all the facts at hand so that you can make the best possible decisions on the way to world domination, Vesper One. I've always believed that and always will. I am here to serve, nothing else."

Mollified, Vesper One said, "What else do I need to know?"

"We captured Isabel's men. But we have not gotten her yet. That means she is around here somewhere."

"Without her men I'm not that worried," replied Vesper One. "She is troublesome, that is all. I trust that the Wyomings have been dealt with?"

Sandy checked his watch and smiled. "The water was programmed to come on several hours ago. I'm certain they're dead. Now, back to Isabel. Obviously her status as Vesper Two can no longer stand. So, I thought . . . ?" He let his voice trail off and looked expectantly at his youthful leader.

"If Chicago is destroyed as planned, you will be elevated to Vesper Two, I give you my word."

Sandy smiled. He didn't believe it, of course. There was no such thing as a Vesper having a word to keep. They all lied, all the time. They would say or do anything to get what they wanted. And being elevated to Vesper Two meant that he had only one more person to eliminate to become the top evildoer. Because he never kept his word, either.

I would have been a remarkable politician, thought Sandy.

"Thank you so much, Vesper One. You will never regret your decision."

"I hope I won't. I don't like regretting decisions. If you don't believe me, just ask Isabel."

The tone and look of Vesper One gave Sandy momentary pause. But then, he shouldn't have been surprised.

He is a homicidal maniac. In fact, we all are.

"I hear you loud and clear, O Great Leader."

He looked at his watch again. "And we now have precisely fifty-seven minutes and fourteen seconds for you to get in that room, insert the gear, and initiate the device. No pressure, just the facts."

Vesper One nodded. "It will be done."

Then his gaze fixed on one of the TV screens.

"Brilliant!"

"What is it?" asked Sandy as he hurried over.

Vesper One pointed with glee at the screen.

There was Isabel, wandering down a tunnel, looking lost and beaten.

Vesper One said, "I think it's time to finish dear Isabel once and for all." He called up his men on his secure phone.

"Kill her," he said. "Now."

Isabel *was* wandering the tunnels, hopelessly lost. One of her men had carried the GPS device that would have allowed her to navigate the tunnels. But the fools had run off and now she was alone. She could not see the embedded cameras, but she could sense that she was being watched.

As she passed one glass-enclosed room, she ducked down. There was a guard in there monitoring several surveillance screens. Isabel peered through the glass and saw images on one of the screens. It was the room with the Doomsday device. She could see it clearly. She could see Amy and Dan, and a wounded Fiske. She smiled gleefully at his bandaged shoulder. Then her gaze went to the far corner of the room, where she saw two bodies under the blankets. One was big and one was small. Then she saw Ian sitting next to the smaller body, crying.

As Isabel watched he drew back the blanket, revealing the face of his dead sister.

Something cracked in Isabel's brain when she saw the image of her dead child. She had killed many people in her life. She had disowned her children for betraying her. She had boasted that she would kill them both if she had to. And she had meant it.

And yet as she looked at dead Natalie and sobbing Ian, Isabel could not seem to remember doing any of those things.

Her child was dead. Someone had killed her. And she knew who had done it.

Vesper One.

Isabel did it before she could even give the decision a second of thought. She dug out the flask from the knapsack she carried, opened it, and drank the contents down to the last drop.

She waited for a moment, unsure of what would happen next.

Had the idiot Dan Cahill made the serum correctly? Would it work? Or would she instead be poisoned? Quite ironic, since she was the queen of poisons.

Five seconds went by and Isabel was on the verge of believing that nothing would happen.

And then, in the blur of an eye, everything happened.

Everything.

CHAPTER 38

"They're probably watching us," Dan whispered to his sister.

"I know. I'm sure this whole complex is wired for surveillance."

"Do you think they'll be coming soon?"

"Soon enough," said Amy.

"We've got four guns and thirteen people. They'll have a lot more than that."

"That's okay. We're always the underdogs. Makes us work harder."

"You're just trying to make me feel better."

"Pretty much, yes."

"Think we can get out of this one, Amy?"

"I think we have as good a shot as anyone. Under the circumstances," she added.

"Quite diplomatic of you," said Fiske, who had been listening.

Amy wasn't really listening to Fiske. She was once more staring up at the Doomsday device. She drew closer.

"Amy, don't get that close," warned Dan. "It might suck you in or something."

Amy was staring at the empty niche where the gear would have to be inserted for the device to fully work.

Dan drew next to her and looked at where she was staring.

"What are you thinking?" he asked.

"I'm thinking that in order for Vesper One to start up this sucker, he's going to have to turn off the 'force field' to insert the gear."

Dan's eyes widened. "You're right. But how does that help us?"

"We'll see," his sister said vaguely. "But with the power off, we might have our chance. Remember we were trying to think of a way to short-circuit it? That way we won't have to. He'll do it for us."

"I hope you're right," said Dan uneasily.

Hamilton called out, "I hear something."

They all froze and listened intently.

Jake said, "They're coming. Everyone get ready." He stepped back from the door, took cover behind some large boxes, and slipped out his gun, aiming it at the doorway.

Hamilton did likewise at the portal he was guarding.

All the others took up various positions of hiding around the room, but in places where they could attack in an instant.

Sinead ran over to Reagan. "Let me have your gun."

"What?"

"Your gun, let me have it."

"Why?"

"I'm a better shot. And you're better fighting with your feet and hands. We all have to play to our strengths."

"The only problem is, I don't trust you," Reagan shot back.

"But I do."

They both turned to see Amy there. She held her gun out to Sinead.

"I trust you, Sinead."

"Are you sure?" asked Sinead, looking surprised. She didn't move to take the weapon.

"I don't have any choice."

Sinead slowly reached out and took the gun.

Reagan gave her gun to Amy. "Sinead is right. Play to our strengths." She raced over to guard another doorway.

Sinead looked at Amy. "I won't disappoint you. I'll fight to the death."

"I know. We all will. We have no choice, really."

The two young women shared a hug and then headed off to different parts of the room.

Amy ran over to where Dan was kneeling behind some boxes. He was smacking his fists together, his eyes rotating among the doors in and out of the room.

Amy knelt next to him, her gaze darting around the room as well.

"This is it," she said.

"Yep," said Dan.

"Wish you had the serum?"

He turned to her, clearly surprised by the question. "No, I'm glad I don't."

"Want to win fair and square?"

"Something like that, yeah."

"What separates us from the Vespers of the world."

"I guess it does."

"Whatever happens, I love you, Dan."

Her eyes grew misty and Dan's did, too.

Brother and sister shared a quick hug.

"I'll see you when it's over," said Dan.

"Yes, you will," replied his sister.

Amy hurried off. She stopped near the device and eyed the empty niche and then her pistol. She listened to the hum of the electricity coming from the device. Then, as she drew closer, she felt something tug hard on her pistol. Surprised, she looked up at the Doomsday device, the idea coming to her in a flash.

If only it could work, she thought.

She ran to the others. "Put the guns down," she said. "And take off any metal you have now." They all looked at her like she was crazy. "Just do it now. Please. It's the only chance we have."

The pistols were placed on the floor and everyone took off any metal they had on.

Amy put the pistol down, ran to one of the crates, threw it open, and pulled out the copper wiring. Carrying it wrapped around her shoulder, she raced back to the device and began to walk around it, unspooling the wire as she did so. She jumped back as the wire flew from her hands and wrapped itself around the device like a mummy's bandages.

Praying that it would work, she ran over to the others, who were staring at her, bewildered, until their pistols and other metal objects started flying off and sticking to the device.

"What have you done, Amy?" screamed Reagan.

"Given us a real chance, I hope."

And then she had no more time to think at all. The distant sounds now became far clearer. And nearer. The battle was about to begin.

The last battle, thought Amy. There was no escape possible this time. It was kill or be killed. She drew a quick breath and waited.

It wouldn't be long now.

The Vespers were coming.

CHAPTER 39

Not one of the three doors was thrown open.

It, of course, could not be that easy.

The walls opened instead, hissing along on motorized tracks

This caught the Cahills momentarily off guard as hordes of screaming Vespers poured through these openings, carrying guns and metal bats.

Then it was the Vespers who were caught off guard.

A dozen of them holding guns were ripped off their feet and flew through the air, landing against the device, sticking to it, and being instantly electrocuted.

"Now!" screamed Amy. "Attack!"

"Charge!" bellowed Fiske as he ran forward.

They clashed in the middle of the room. Many of the Vespers had realized that the device had been turned into a giant electromagnet and had hastily dropped their weapons before they zoomed off to attach to the machine. But there weren't as many Vespers as before. And they couldn't use guns.

Or knives, as one found out when he pulled a long

blade and tried to slash Sinead with it. He was catapulted over her and landed upside down against the device.

All thirteen of the Cahills fought like demons. Despite his injuries, Fiske kicked and punched like an enraged beast.

Hamilton, Jake, and Reagan mowed down Vesper after Vesper, using all of their strength and fighting skill.

Amy and Dan once more stood back-to-back, punching and kicking all Vespers who came near them. Even Atticus and Ted were swinging and kicking, although they often didn't hit anything other than themselves.

Amy watched with pride as Sinead slammed into two Vespers who were on the verge of strangling Nellie, knocking both of them unconscious.

Jonah was racing around, kicking and singing a cappella, timing his kicks with pitch-perfect crescendos.

Phoenix was the first to go down under the sheer weight of the Vespers, who kept crowding into the room.

Little by little the Cahills were pushed back. They finally formed a circle in the middle of the room, and stood fighting side by side.

Jake and Amy found themselves shoulder to shoulder. They glanced at each other during a brief break in the battle.

"How you holding up, Ames?" he asked.

"Been better. You?"

"Could use some downtime."

"Maybe we can go somewhere warm after this is over."

"Yeah, maybe we can."

"We're going to die, aren't we?" asked Amy.

"Probably, but we're going to take as many of them with us as possible," answered Jake.

"I like your style."

"Back at you."

"ENOUGH!"

The voice boomed throughout the room and everyone suddenly froze in mid-punch and kick.

Vesper One and Sandy entered the room. Sandy was pulling along a wooden cart on which rested a large wooden case.

The Vespers parted, allowing Vesper One to come forward, where he stood a few feet from his circle of opponents. He looked at Amy.

"It's over," he said calmly. "And you've lost."

"Who says?" asked Amy.

"He said," snapped Sandy. "And he's Vesper One. And I'm Vesper Two. And if you don't mind, we're on a tight schedule. We're planning to destroy Chicago and we have to get a move on."

Vesper One said, "So it's time for the Cahills to admit defeat. Give up now and you will be spared. Resist further and every one of you will die a horrible death. You have ten seconds to decide."

Amy and the others looked around at one another.

Actually, they were all looking at her. She stood tall, put up her fists, and said, "I'll take the horrible death, you freak."

All the others put their fists up, too, and prepared to fight on.

"Have it your way," said Vesper One. "Mercy isn't really my thing, anyway." He turned to Sandy. "Hand out the stone clubs."

Sandy opened the crate he had rolled in and began to hand out long clubs that had wooden handles and heavy stone ends.

When each of his men had a weapon, Vesper One looked at Amy and said, "I'm thrilled to be able to fulfill your last wish of dying a horrible death." He turned to his followers. "Kill them. Now!"

Before a single Vesper could move, one of the doors to the chamber was blasted open by the force of six other Vespers being thrown through it.

What came through the door after them made everyone in the room, even Vesper One, take a long step back.

Isabel stood before them. She looked the same and yet she looked different. There was something ethereal about her movements. She seemed to be floating a few inches above the floor. It was as though she were no longer confined by the physical properties of the Earth. And if one looked closely she seemed fairly red in the face, almost like she had a bad sunburn.

Dan looked at Amy. "Wow. It really did work."

She hissed, "She's red! What did you put in the serum?"

"Exactly what I was supposed to. Well, and some red M&M's for taste. You think that's where the red color came from?"

A bloodcurdling scream escaping Isabel's lips, she raced toward the outer circle of Vespers with such speed that it caught all of them unprepared. She smashed into the front row of Vespers with such force that it knocked ten of them head over heels across the room. Others threw their clubs at her, but she effortlessly dodged most of them, her body spinning and contorting in the most amazing ways and utilizing jaw-dropping angles and gymnastic ability. The ones she didn't dodge she caught and sent flying back at their original owners with the velocity of a bullet and dead-on aim, dropping them all. She next lifted up three Vespers, their feet dangling ten feet above the floor, and threw them across the room, where they hit the far wall and fell to the floor, dead.

Sandy had already made a run for the door, his face pale, his expression panicked.

He ran right into a still-soaked Cheyenne and Casper, who were coming through the doorway. They snagged the intrepid, if diabolical, weatherman and carried him off kicking and screaming.

Casper said nastily, "Just the scumball we wanted to run into."

Meanwhile, like a flesh-and-bone meat cleaver,

Isabel raced through the ranks of the Vespers, kicking, punching, and catapulting through the air. With each blow a Vesper fell, while any attempts to land a solid strike against her failed. She was too fast, too nimble, and too quick-thinking. She seemed to know what the Vespers were going to do before they even did it. She was like a dozen perfect fighting machines rolled into one.

Vesper One turned and ran toward the Doomsday device.

Amy saw this and raced after him, Dan on her heels.

Jake, Sinead, and all the others ran away from Isabel's approach and hid behind some crates. From there they watched as Vespers flew around the room, crashing and dying as Isabel tore through them.

When all the Vespers were vanquished, Isabel stopped and turned to the body of her daughter. She sailed over to her, lifted off the blanket, and stared down at Natalie. And for one instant Isabel looked closer to a human being than she ever had. Then she put the blanket back and turned to stare at Vesper One, the degree of hatred in her eyes awful to behold.

Amy and Dan were within feet of him, blocking his escape.

Vesper One was not looking at them, or Isabel. His attention was on the Doomsday device. In his hand was the gear. In his other hand was a remote-control device.

With a flick, he turned off the electrical power. The

DAY OF DOOM

259

machine powered down and all the Vespers and metal stuck to it immediately fell to the floor.

He rushed forward, the gear poised in his hand.

"Oh, no you don't!" screamed Amy.

She and Dan flew forward to stop him from inserting the last gear.

But an instant later they were hurled to the side as Isabel pushed past them with astonishing speed.

She collided with Vesper One right as he reached the device. He stretched out and placed the gear in the niche. The device started to glow with power, even as Isabel and Vesper One fought each other.

In another instant they were both sucked toward the device as it came on full power.

"LOOK OUT!" screamed Sinead.

The walls and ceiling of the room began to shake. Bits of rock tumbled down and hit the floor, creating small craters.

The power surge in the device became stronger.

As Amy and Dan watched from a distance, Vesper One was caught between Isabel and the device. He was slowly and inexorably being crushed between the unstoppable force and the immovable object.

When he realized this seconds later, he panicked. But by then it was too late.

The walls and ceiling began to shake more and more, as if an earthquake was happening. Huge chunks of rock were now falling from the walls and ceiling.

Jake grabbed Amy and Dan. "We've got to get out of here. The whole mountain is coming down," he screamed.

Amy, Dan, and the others dodged tumbling rocks as they raced to the doorway.

Amy yelled, "But what about the Doomsday device? We have to stop it."

Fiske's calming voice reached her. "I think we just did. Look!"

Amy shot a glance at the device. Vesper One appeared to have melted right into the thing. It seemed that his face was now part of the machine.

Meanwhile, Isabel was ripping at the device, tearing off huge chunks of it with her superpowered hands. The machine started to misfire, sending out massive surges of electrical energy. And then it started to shake uncontrollably as Isabel continued to rip it apart.

As he ran, Fiske looked back and yelled, "She's destroying it. But I think it's going to blow any second."

A few seconds later, an enormous explosion occurred, lifting Amy off her feet. An instant before that happened, all Amy could remember seeing was the device, Vesper One, and Isabel Kabra disintegrate into dust. The entire room shook once more, and then everything went black.

CHAPTER 40

The first person Amy saw was her mother. She smiled and hugged her daughter, and spoke words that Amy had a hard time hearing. Then her father appeared next to her. His smile warmed every molecule in Amy's body. And that was good because she felt so cold. *Sooo* cold.

Am I dead?

When Grace Cahill sat down next to her and took her hand, Amy knew that she was no longer in the land of the living.

"How did it happen?" she asked her grandmother.

"You fought the good fight, Amy. You defeated the Vespers. It just came at a great personal cost."

Amy nodded. She tried to remain calm even as her chest felt tight and the tears trickled down her cheeks.

"But Dan's okay, right? He made it? Right?"

Grace pointed around the misty edges of the space they were in.

"You don't see your little brother here, do you?"

Relief washed over Amy. At least Dan had

survived. He would carry on the Cahill name and family. Attleboro would be his home. He would grow up and have kids, and maybe he would name one of his daughters Amy.

With that thought more tears clustered around Amy's eyes.

It sucks being morbid.

But she couldn't help herself. She was dead, after all. She had the right to be a little depressed, to wallow in a little self-pity.

She looked around. Jake wasn't here, either. He had made it, too. Maybe he and Sinead would fall in love, marry, have kids, grow old together.

Okay, Amy, enough with the tear ducts.

"Hi, Amy."

She looked up to see Evan there. He looked just like he always looked, except a bit pale, which being dead can certainly do to a person. Amy supposed she looked like parchment herself.

"Hi, Evan."

He said sheepishly, "Kind of a bummer, being dead and all."

"Yeah," she said. "But it could be worse."

"How's that?"

"We could be dead and the world could have ended thanks to Vesper One."

"Hey, I died before it all turned out. So we won?"

Amy nodded. "Yeah, we stopped the machine. Isabel took the serum and went all *Matrix* on us. She squashed Vesper One like a bug and died in the process. The planet will live on, even if we won't."

"That's cool. Maybe we can hang out together."

"That would be nice, Evan. Thanks."

Amy glanced to her left and caught a breath. She was seeing something she thought she never would.

Isabel Kabra was walking along with Natalie. Hand in hand.

Isabel looked different. She looked, well, normal, not evil. Natalie was staring up at her mother as they walked along. She looked happy. Happy to be dead.

Wow, thought Amy. *Like, really, wow.*

Off in another corner she saw Alistair. It looked to her like he was running some sort of business. But dead people didn't buy things. Or eat things. What would have been the point?

"Amy? AMY?"

Things went black again.

"Amy?"

Something shook her by the arm. Amy slowly opened her eyes.

The misty room was gone. The sun was shining in a window. She felt a breeze on her face. She sat up, looked around.

She was in her bedroom at Attleboro.

"Amy?"

She turned to see Dan sitting on the side of her bed and looking at her anxiously.

"Dan? What's going on? Am I dead?"

Dan smiled. "You almost were. In fact, we thought you were, but we were wrong, thank goodness."

"What happened?"

"To make a long story short, the mountain sort of collapsed. We barely got out. You got hit in the head by a chunk of rock."

Amy reached up and felt the bandage around her head.

"They had to cut some of your hair off, but it'll grow back fast."

"I don't really remember."

"Docs said short-term amnesia is perfectly normal for getting your head creamed like that. It might come back. But then again, you might not want it to."

"What happened after the mountain collapsed?"

"Jake carried you over his shoulder the rest of the way."

"Jake did? Is he okay?" she added quickly.

"Everyone's okay. Well, everyone else. You remember about Natalie and Evan?"

Amy sat back against her pillow. She blinked back tears. "I was hoping that was a dream."

Was I dead? I saw Evan. And Natalie. Did I just come back from almost dying?

"We got you to a hospital. It was touch and go for a while."

"I just don't remember any of it."

"You had surgery and were released last week. It'll take you a while to get your strength back, but the docs said you'll be fine. No permanent damage."

"And what about the Doomsday device?"

"Buried under the mountain. Along with Isabel and Vesper One, if anything was left of them."

"And the Wyomings and Sandy?"

"Arrested. For multiple felonies. Kidnapping. Assault. Unlawful imprisonment. Stealing a truck. Driving a stolen truck without a license. Oh, and trying to blow up the world. That was a biggie. And they also got Sandy, for impersonating a meteorologist. Seems that he never actually got his degree and he forged his credentials."

"And Nellie and Fiske? Their injuries?"

"Doing fine." He paused. "Oh, and I forgot. Chicago is still there."

Amy smiled. "Maybe we should go visit again. By train. It was a lot of fun."

"I think I'll go by plane," replied Dan. "And meet you there."

A week later, after she felt stronger, Amy met with everyone at Attleboro.

She hugged Ian and talked to him about Natalie and their mother. She told Ian that she had seen Isabel's face when she had spotted Natalie's body.

"I think she really cared for you two," said Amy. "Deep, deep down."

Ian seemed comforted by this.

Sinead was with Ted and Ned. Both of them looked better and Sinead reported that some experimental treatments undertaken in Switzerland were really starting to pay dividends.

"Thank goodness I didn't try to use the serum," she said. "Nasty stuff. I even felt a little sorry for Isabel."

Amy said, "I'm looking forward to being friends with you again, Sinead. And all of the medical treatments Ted and Ned require will be taken care of."

"That's not your problem, Amy. It's my burden to deal with."

"It's *our* issue to deal with, Sinead. We are family, after all."

"But after all the things I did?"

"We all make mistakes, Sinead. But there is a thing called redemption. You fought with us against the Vespers. You saved my life. You saved Nellie's life. You're a good person. Never stop believing that."

Sinead looked uneasily at her, swallowed with difficulty, and gave her a hug.

In one corner of the room Phoenix and Jonah were doing a little jam session on the piano. It turned out that Phoenix actually had better pipes than his famous relative.

Jonah said, "Okay, little bro, some mentoring, some

attitude and clothing changes, and you learn my hip-hop version of the moonwalk, we got a gold-plated show we take on the road."

Dan stood behind Jonah and mouthed frantically to Phoenix, *Just say NO!*

Hamilton and Reagan were in one corner of the room practicing their martial skills.

"Couldn't have done it without both of you," Amy told them.

Hamilton said, "Just think of the stories we'll have to tell our kids. Saved the world. Not that many people can say they did that."

"Drop and give me twenty, Ham," said his sister, "You're looking a little soft."

Nellie looked beautiful and her shoulder and arm hung normally. She'd cut her hair and it was now dyed a new color that Amy could not really describe. They hugged and Nellie said she was going to take a little vacation from being their guardian. "Just need to get my mojo back. And I got cheated on my Paris trip, so I'm booking a trip now that I know you're okay."

Fiske was dressed all in black. With his fine, silver-white hair he cut quite a figure. "I don't think you and Dan need guardians anymore," he said.

"Maybe not, but we do need family, right?" said Amy.

"Are you asking me to stick around?" said Fiske.

Amy looked at Nellie and then back at Fiske. "I'm asking both of you to hang with us till we drive you absolutely crazy. Although with Dan in the picture that might be tomorrow," she added, smiling.

Fiske bowed deeply. "It would be my honor."

"Mine, too," said Nellie. "As soon as I get back from Paris."

"Fair enough," said a grinning Amy.

That left Atticus, who Amy spent time with and gave plenty of hugs, too.

Then there was Jake.

"We have a lot to talk about, I guess," Jake said.

"We do, but we don't have to do it now."

"I'm really sorry about Evan. He was a cool dude."

"Yes, he was. And we'll never forget him because he'll always be a part of us."

She took his hand. "And by the way, thanks for carrying me out of that mountain."

"Any time," he replied, smiling at her.

"And I think I owe you something from the storage room at the train station in Chicago."

She reached up on tiptoe and kissed him.

Later, Dan and Amy walked over the lovely grounds of Attleboro. This was Cahill land, something that was intimate and comforting and familiar. They walked to the top of a little knoll and looked out at a place that their family had called home for so long.

Amy said, "I thought I was dead, you know. I saw Mom and Dad and Grace. And everyone else who had passed. I guess it was just a dream. But it seemed so real."

"Did part of you want to stay there?" Dan asked curiously.

"Yes, but it was just a little part. Most of me wanted to come back here, to the living."

"I'm glad you did. It would've been pretty lonely around here without you."

They walked some more and then headed back to the house.

"So, I guess we can settle down to nice quiet lives now," said Amy. "I can think about college, you'll be going into high school soon. Just . . . normal . . . every-day . . . lives." With these last words her tone grew rote and her expression became bored.

"Yeah, what a relief," said Dan, but he looked every bit as bored as his sister.

They looked at each other.

Dan said, "Normal everyday lives? Sounds so cheesy, doesn't it?"

Amy nodded. "Of course it does. And you know why, right?"

"Why?" asked Dan.

She grinned. "We're Cahills. We save the world. It's what we do."

"It's what we do," repeated Dan and he grinned, too.

They gripped each other's hands and started to sprint toward the house.